HAND-TO-HAND SHOWDOWN

The Comanche twisted around, whipped his knife from his breechclout, and charged toward his enemy. Bolt raised his own knife and aimed for the Indian's heart. The scout ducked sideways just as Bolt stabbed with the glinting weapon. Blood spurted from the long, deep gash in the brave's arm. Bolt had missed his mark,

The scout stood in front of Bolt, legs spread, sweat glistening on his bronze body, his black hair straight and scraggly. His dark eyes glittered as he grinned evilly. The renegade held his knife up, taunting Bolt with his movement. Then, with a blood-curdling shriek, the Indian lunged.

WHITE SQUAW
Zebra's Adult Western Series
by E. J. Hunter

BOLT #25

HOT ON THE WARPATH

BY
CORT MARTIN

ZEBRA BOOKS
KENSINGTON PUBLISHING CORP.

ZEBRA BOOKS

are published by

Kensington Publishing Corp.
475 Park Avenue South
New York, NY 10016

First printing: January 1988

Printed in the United States of America

CHAPTER ONE

The silence across the land was almost unbearable.

"Hear that thunder?" Tom Penrod asked.

Jared Bolt glanced up from the pair of buckets he and Tom were filling with water so they could wash the breakfast and lunch dishes. Bared to the waist on the hot spring day, the two friends dipped water from the rain barrels out back of their ranch house and set the buckets over the fire to heat the water. Out in the pasture, the cattle grazed in belly-high grass.

Bolt tilted his head back and scanned the wide expanse of clear blue sky.

"What thunder, Tom? Far as I can see, there ain't a cloud in the sky."

"The thunder of them damned noisy grasshoppers and locusts out in the fields. Sounds like a herd of stampeding buffalo." Tom clamped his hands over his ears, as if to shut out the deafening racket of the constantly buzzing insects.

Bolt laughed. "I know what you mean. It's

been quiet as hell this week with all but one of the harlots gone. Not that they make that much noise when they're here, but I've gotten used to having them around."

"I wouldn't mind bachin' it for a spell if it weren't for all these damned dirty dishes," Tom grumbled. "Look at those grimy, black pots, and Harmony always keeps 'em lookin' like they was brand new."

"There's just some things a woman can do better than a fellow, Tom, and dishes is one of them. Harmony's got us spoiled rotten, you know, the way she picks up after us, and cleans the house and cooks for us."

"She's some woman, Bolt. You really ought to marry that gal." Tom glanced over at his friend.

"That's what she keeps telling me," Bolt laughed as he grabbed a tea towel. "Your turn to wash."

"I don't know how Harmony does it all and still has the energy to serve as the happy madam at our bordello every evening. Hell, I'm tired just looking at this mess of dishes."

Tom tested the water and poured some of it into the two large metal basins that were built into a long plank counter. Since Harmony usually did the dishes in the kitchen of the ranch house, the basins were primarily used for scrubbing dirty clothes, with the aid of a washboard. Bolt and Tom used the basins for washing up before meals when they were through with the chores that came with the cattle-raising busi-

6

ness. They also used the counter and wash basins for cleaning fish and small game. They had rigged up a shower a few feet away from the counter, and when there wasn't enough rain to fill the large barrels, they hauled water from the nearby stream.

The wash area was down the hill from the main ranch house where they lived, near the crude wooden stairway that led up the hill to the house. Way beyond the wash area stood their popular Rocking Bar Bordello, a two-story log cabin with a big living room where the men in need gathered, and six bedrooms upstairs where the harlots slept. Out behind the large log-cabin bordello were six separate, one-room cottages where the soiled doves took those men who paid for their pleasure. Across the wide expanse of ankle-deep green grass from the bordello was the stable, and beyond that, the bunkhouse where the two cowhands, Chet and Rusty, bedded down.

Bolt shook his head. "I don't mind doin' these dishes, but we got us a heap of dirty clothes to wash in the morning and I ain't lookin' forward to that miserable, back-breaking, knuckle-scraping chore. Hell, it's an all-day affair."

"That's what you get for giving the girls a long Easter holiday," Tom smirked. "Hell, I tried to tell you we shouldn't have let all the gals go waltzing off at the same time."

"Tom, it doesn't really matter if most of the girls are taking their well-earned vacation at the same time. Harmony's the only one who keeps house for us. And just remember," Bolt said with a smug grin, "Harmony will be gone a week longer than the other girls, so you'd better get used to your fingers looking like shriveled up prunes."

"And you remember this, my friend," Tom said with an equally smug smile. "When the harlots come traipsing back here to work after their merry holidays and you open up the Rocking Bar Bordello for business again, you're not going to have a madam to run the place until Harmony gets back. What're you gonna do? Dress up in one of her frilly gowns that'll show your hairy cleavage and play the part of a madam? I can see you now," he laughed. He slid a stack of the dirty dishes into the warm water and began to scrub the top plate with a dish rag.

"No, Tom, I thought I'd leave that little job to you. You ain't got no hair on your chest anyway."

"The hell you say!" Tom dipped the clean plate into the rinse water and set it down on the counter.

Bolt picked the plate up, let it drip for a minute, then began to dry it. "With your sweet disposition, I think you'd make a charming madam and hostess at the bordello, Tom. And I know the girls would love to fuss over you, putting your makeup on. Not much they could do with that mop of hair you've got, but they might put a pretty red ribbon in it for you."

Tom ignored Bolt's teasing. "Well, I still say it

was foolish to shut the bordello down for a week when you could have let the girls go away one at a time and still kept the place open for business. Just think of all the money we're losing this week."

"We aren't greedy, and we ain't desperate for money, Tom. The cattle ranch is paying its way."

"I know," Tom put a washed and rinsed platter on the counter.

"And you also know that the girls needed the time off. Those girls have worked hard for us."

"With good pay," Tom added.

"You're damned right, with good pay. They deserve every penny they earn and they also deserve some time away from here."

"I ain't sayin' they don't, but I still don't see why you don't let Linda Ramsey do the cooking and cleaning for us," Tom said as he concentrated on a particularly dirty bowl. He dipped the bowl in rinse water, then set it aside for Bolt to dry. "She offered and her cooking's a hell of a lot more tolerable than yours."

"Because it's Linda's vacation time, too," Bolt said firmly. He picked up the bowl, saw that it was still dirty and slipped it back into Tom's dishwater. "She chose to stay here and catch up on her sewing instead of visiting friends or kin, and I ain't askin' her to lift a hand this week. She's already cooked two nice big suppers for us since the other girls have been gone, so I don't know what you're complaining about."

"Because you won't let her do all the cooking,

9

even though she's willing. And because I'm tired of eating beef that tastes like the hide of a tough old buffalo." Tom rewashed the bowl, rinsed it and slammed it down on the wooden plank of the counter. "That clean enough now?" he said sarcastically.

"Quite. You're sure in a pleasant mood today. You got a burr in your britches, Tom?"

"Forget it," Tom snapped. "It's just that Linda sits over there in that big old house all by herself, lonesome as hell, when she could be over here with us, helping us wash these damned dishes."

"Linda chose to stay here where she could have some peace and quiet, and some privacy, Tom. And as far as I know, she ain't that lonesome at night. You make sure of that."

Tom glanced over at Bolt, a shy grin on his face. "Why do you think she wanted to stay here? Besides, it wouldn't be gentlemanly to let her stay alone in that big old house all night. I'm just protecting her."

"Nice to know you're so considerate, Tom."

The two men stood side-by-side, doing the dishes in silence for a few minutes.

"You know, it does seem quiet and deserted out here today," Bolt sighed. "Especially with Chet and Rusty gone to town." He dried a wine goblet, held it up to the light and studied it, then brought it back down and wiped the smudges from the rim with a fresh, dry dish towel.

"Ain't it clean enough for you?" Tom snarled.

"Yeah, it's clean."

"That's another thing," Tom said. "I don't see why you sent Chet and Rusty to San Antonio for supplies today. You and I usually do that."

"Ahh ha," Bolt smiled. "So that's what you're pouting about. You didn't get to go to town today and flirt with all the pretty young ladies who stroll the boardwalk."

"I ain't pouting. It's just that with the girls gone, everything seems different. It's too damned quiet around here."

"You should be damned thankful for that, but I agree. Look, Tom, the other girls will be back day after tomorrow and then we can eat our meals with them. And I think we'll both survive the housework until Harmony gets back."

A cow bellowed from someplace out on the back forty acres of their prairieland pasture. Beyond that, a dog barked.

"Hark! I hear voices!" Tom cocked his head and listened. Water dripped down his arm as he raised a hand to his ear.

"A cow and a dog?" Bolt laughed. "Does that excite you, Tom?"

Tom snapped his wet fingers and they didn't make a sound. "Aww, shucks," he grinned. "I thought it was some sexy siren beckoning me to her lair."

"I think your mind's going, Tom."

"Yep. Wouldn't doubt it. I heard that if you keep your hands in water too long, it affects the brain."

11

Another distant cry penetrated the silence of the prairie. The same faraway dog yapped, but Bolt knew damned well the loud mournful howl was not that of a bawling cow in the pasture. It was a shrill wailing sound. A female's scream, he thought.

His first thoughts were of Linda Ramsey, and he wondered if she had ridden out to the rolling, wooded stretch of the pasture. Despite the heat of the afternoon, a chill ran up his spine and caused the fine hairs at the nape of his neck to rise.

"What in the hell was that?" Tom said as he jerked his head around and stared across the land beyond the stable and the bordello. "It sure wasn't the cattle squalling this time."

"I'm not sure." Bolt scanned the sun-drenched countryside, then peered into the dark shadows of the tree-shaded land. "Eerie, whatever it was. A coyote, maybe?"

"That was a woman's scream, wasn't it, Bolt? I'm sure of it."

"Linda?" Bolt ventured. "You think that's Linda out there?"

"No, that's not Linda." Tom shook his head and grabbed for a towel to dry his hands. "I just talked to her a few minutes ago and she's busy sewing up a new gown for herself. Maybe you're right. Maybe it was just a coyote."

"Yeah." Bolt's shoulders sagged with relief. "I guess we're both spooked by the quietness out here today. But that's why we picked this place to settle down, isn't it? The peacefulness?"

"Right," Tom said as he stuck his hands back into the dishwater.

The wailing sound arose again out of the distant land and shattered the silence. Louder this time. Closer. A single, haunting wail, followed by a shrill, discernible cry for help.

Both men took off at a dead run across the yard, heading for the pasture, Tom's hands dripping wet, Bolt's hands filled with the dish towel and a china plate. Other cows bawled and the dog barked more urgently.

"There it is, over there," Bolt said, pointing with the hand that held the dish towel.

"I see it," Tom said as he shielded his eyes from the sun.

Bolt squinted his eyes and watched the covered wagon come up over the horizon, lumbering slowly through the high grass as the horse pulling the wagon struggled to get over the hill. A woman on horseback rode slightly ahead of the wagon, her long, earth-colored skirt flared out over her animal's flanks. Her large, floppy hat bounced with each step the horse took. Judging from the way she slumped in the saddle, Bolt figured her to be an older woman. Trotting along beside the woman's horse, barking his annoyance at her intrusion, was Benji, one of Bolt's herd dogs.

"What the hell?" Tom said. "Why's that old lady riding across our private property instead of using the road like everybody else does? She's got no damned business plowing through our cattle that way."

"I don't know, Tom," Bolt said calmly. "Maybe she's lost."

"That's no excuse. She's scarin' the cattle." Tom wiped his hands on his pants.

The woman spotted them and cracked the leather reins over her horse's neck. She sat up taller in the saddle and rode on ahead of the covered wagon, waving her arm frantically. "Help! Help!" she yelled. Her shrill voice had a dry husk to it.

"Oh oh, I smell trouble heading our way." Tom winced.

Bolt dashed back and set the plates and towel on the plank counter, then strolled up to Tom and watched the woman ride toward them at a gallop.

"Trouble, yes," Bolt said. "But she's obviously the one who's got trouble, Tom. Not us."

"That's what you always say, Bolt, but every damned time you try to help some poor damsel in distress, it seems we're the ones who end up ass deep in trouble."

"Only when she's young and pretty," Bolt grinned slyly. As the woman rode closer, he tried to get a glimpse of her face, but it was hidden in the shadows of her floppy hat.

"Someday, I wish you'd learn to turn your back on the women who come to you with that poor, innocent, helpless look in their eyes."

"Hey, wait a minute, Tom. You've already got

14

me deeply involved with this old bat and we don't even know who she is or what she wants. Where's your sense of humanity?"

"In my britches," Tom said sullenly. "Along with the burr and my sweet disposition."

Bolt looked over at his friend, a frown creasing his brow. "You worry me, Tom. You ain't usually this cantankerous after you're had your morning coffee. You feeling all right?"

"Yeah."

"Help me! Please help me," the woman yelled from twenty yards away, her voice hoarse and weak. The horse faltered briefly, throwing the woman off balance. She clutched at the saddle horn with one hand and reached for her floppy brown hat with the other. Instead of grabbing her hat, she knocked it from her head. Long, raven-dark hair, matted and straggly, tumbled free from its trap and framed her dirt-smudged face.

Bolt stared at her in awe as she barreled toward them. She was much younger than he'd expected, twenty, he'd guess. And as she reined her horse to a dirt-spraying halt in front of him, the dog still yapping at the stranger, Bolt saw that the girl had a thin, pretty face beneath the dirt.

"Hush, Benji," Bolt commanded. The dog looked up at him, wagged its tail, gave one final bark, then turned and slunk away, his tail tucked between his legs.

A sudden shiver coursed through the young

girl's body and then her shoulders sagged. Her body seemed to go limp all over, although she still clutched the reins tightly in her hands, as if she couldn't move them. For a long moment, she just sat in the saddle and stared down at Bolt, a blank, glazed-over expression in her dark, deep-set eyes.

"Good afternoon, ma'am," Bolt said as he tipped his hat. He saw the trail dust and the dark stains on the simple, light brown frock she wore and wondered how long she'd been riding across the prairie. She looked in tough shape.

"Where am I?" the woman asked, a bewildered look on her face.

"You're trespassing, that's where you are," Tom blurted out. He turned slightly and pointed across the expanse of lawn and up the hill, to the trail beyond the front of the ranch house. "You ride straight on through our property to the road right up there," he told the girl. "Turn left and San Antonio's two miles north of here."

Bolt shot Tom a dirty look and then stepped in front of him. "You're at the Rocking Bar Ranch, ma'am," he said gently.

The young woman continued to stare at Bolt with vacant eyes, as if she hadn't heard either one of them.

"Are you lost, ma'am?" he asked. There was no response except the woman seemed to clutch the reins even tighter. "Are you all right, lady?" he called out. "Ma'am! Miss!"

Still, she didn't answer.

Bolt shuddered, suddenly extremely uneasy about the way the stranger stared at him with cold, lifeless eyes. And yet he couldn't take his eyes off hers.

CHAPTER TWO

"Miss!" Bolt called again. "Miss, are you all right?" He waved his arms in front of him, trying to startle the young woman out of her trance. He watched her dark, vacant eyes for some sign of life, some flicker of emotion or awareness.

Suddenly the bedraggled girl sat straight up in the saddle, a stunned look on her face, her death-like grip on the reins relaxing a bit. She reached up and touched the dark tangles of her matted hair, patted her head, as if looking for her floppy hat.

"Where am I?" she asked again. This time she looked directly at Bolt instead of staring through him with unseeing eyes.

Before he could answer, she jerked her head around, glanced from side to side, and peered across the yard in front of her, her face clouded with panic. "Where's Mama?" she shrieked. "And Aunt Sophie? Where are they?"

"Are they in that wagon back there?" Bolt nodded toward the open pasture behind the young woman.

He walked a few feet beyond her and scooped her hat up off the ground, dusted it off. When he handed it up to her, he glanced out in the pasture and saw the covered wagon inching toward them. When he had first spotted the spring wagon looming out of the distance, he had assumed that the person who rode on the high driver's seat was a man, clad in dark clothing. Now that the wagon was closer, he saw that it was a woman, wearing a black, high-necked dress, who sat in the driver's seat. Reins in hand, the woman sat tall and rigid on the seat as she guided the bouncing wagon around the ruts in the ground.

The girl twisted around in her saddle, glanced over her shoulder. "Oh, thank God, they're still with me," she sighed. She took her hat from Bolt and stuffed it behind the saddle. "For a minute, I thought they'd been captured."

Bolt looked up at young woman and saw the wild, feral look in her dark eyes, like that of a trapped animal. He wondered if she was in her right mind.

"Ma'am, are you lost?" he asked.

"No, I just don't know where I am."

"You've stumbled onto the Rocking Bar Ranch. We're two miles south of San Antonio, if that's where you and your kin are headed."

"San Antonio? I didn't realize we'd come so far. But that's not where we're headed. I really don't know where we're going," she said, her wide, searching eyes full of terror. "Just someplace far,

far away."

"Far away from what?" Bolt frowned and again wondered about her sanity. He could see that she was distraught, but she wasn't making any sense.

"Who are you, lady?" Tom asked as he walked up and stood beside Bolt. "And what are you women running away from?"

"My name's Veronica Morningstar, but that doesn't matter right now. You've got to help us. Oh, please help us."

Bolt saw the pleading desperation in the young woman's eyes, the panic, as she eyed both of them.

"What're you needin' help with?"

"We're in need of a place to rest for a spell," Miss Morningstar said, her voice cracking, as if she were trying to control her emotions and keep herself from falling apart completely. "Just a place to rest. We're so tired."

"How long have you been riding?"

"I don't know. Five or six days now. We've had little sleep. Not much food." Suddenly, Veronica brought her hands up and covered her mouth. Her body trembled as she closed her eyes and fought back the tears. "Oh, it was just so terrible, so ghastly." She took a deep breath, then continued. "The Indians attacked us. Killed our menfolk. Took my sister. Chased after us," she gasped. "They're still after us. We have to keep riding. But we've got to stop and rest. Can't go on."

"Calm down, miss. You're all right now," Bolt said. "You say you were attacked by Indians?"

"Yes," she sobbed. "Murdering Comanches. They raided our little village."

"Where?"

"Uvalde. Our village is near Uvalde."

"That's quite a ride from here," Bolt said. "I can understand why you're weary."

"We didn't even know what direction we were headed half the time." Veronica shook her head. "When we saw those wild Indian warriors chasing after us, we knew that we just had to keep riding away from our village, as far as we could, so they wouldn't catch us like they did my sister. I know Heather's dead by now, too."

"How many Indians were there?"

"About ten or twelve of them attacked our village, but we think there are only two of them chasing after us."

"I doubt that they're still chasing you, ma'am," Tom said. "Not this close to civilization."

"Mama thought she spotted one of them yesterday morning." An involuntary shiver coursed through Veronica's body. "That's why we couldn't stop and rest when we needed to. We just knew we had to keep going, no matter what."

"I don't think you have to worry about the Indians any more, Miss Morningstar," Bolt said in a soothing voice. "If they were chasing you, they would have already caught up with you."

"That's right," Tom said. "That covered wagon of yours is too big to hide from the Indians and it's far too slow and bulky to outrun them."

"Not only that," Bolt added, "Comanches are good trackers and they would have found you if they had really wanted to. I think you're safe now."

"Oh, I hope you're right. I've been so scared." She relaxed and looked directly down at Bolt. "Please don't think I'm a dumb, whining, helpless woman, because I'm not. I'm just overcome by grief and the horror I've witnessed."

"I understand," Bolt said.

"The Indians just came out of nowhere. They went on a killing rampage, murdering everyone they could find in our village," Veronica said, as if she had a sudden need to talk about it. "When Papa saw the smoke from a neighbor's farm, he and my brother Tommy were going to ride over and help the Mitchells. But right away, he heard the Indian war cries and then he saw the Comanches coming around the bend toward our farm."

"How do you know they were Comanches?" Tom asked.

"Because Papa told us. Aunt Sophie and I were working out in the garden when it happened, and Mama was standing there talking to us. She was wearing her good black dress 'cause she and Papa were fixing to ride to the cemetery for the burial services of old man Rankin. My poor sister, Heather, was in the house. When Papa saw those Comanches, he told us to run and hide in the barn."

"Didn't your sister go to the barn with you?"

Bolt asked.

Veronica shuddered. "Heather started out the back door, but the Indians came so fast, I guess she got scared and went back inside. And then there was all this horrible confusion. We heard the Indians whooping and hollering and we heard the gunshots, and the screams and moans." She paused and closed her eyes, batted back the tears that spilled over her lids and streaked her dirty cheeks.

"It's all right, Miss Morningstar," Bolt said. "You don't have to tell us about it."

"I want to," she said quietly as she wiped the tears from her eyes. "When it got quiet again, we peeked out of the barn and saw all the dead bodies strewn across the yard. And then we saw some of the Indians riding toward the house with torches in their hands. That's how Aunt Sophie got hurt."

"Did she get burned?" Tom asked.

"No, she made a dash for the house. She knew they were going to burn it down and she wanted to get Heather out of there. Heather saw her coming and ran out the back door at the same time the Indians threw the torches at the house. Mama and I just stood there and watched in horror. We were too stunned by all the killings to move. I tried, but my legs were already shaking and they just wouldn't move. I feel I let my sister down. And Aunt Sophie."

"You were in shock," Bolt said. "That often happens when a person witnesses such brutality as you did."

"But Aunt Sophie was brave enough to try to save Heather, and she got hurt real bad. Three warriors swooped down on them when Heather and Aunt Sophie were running back to the barn. One of the Indians grabbed Heather up and rode off with her. The other two went after Aunt Sophie. One of them threw a tomahawk at her. It missed her head, but hit her in the shoulder. That's where she's hurting the most. The other one rode by and clubbed her on the other shoulder. He must have thought she was dead when she dropped to the ground because he just rode off."

"How deep did the tomahawk go?" Bolt asked.

"I don't know. It hit her and then fell to the ground. She's got a big gash in her back and bruises all over her. And she lost a lot of blood. Mama and I took care of Aunt Sophie as best we could, but I don't know if she's still alive. She was real weak the last time I checked her about an hour ago. She needs to rest so badly without being bounced around."

"How'd you escape the Indians?" Tom asked.

"Mama and I waited until everything was quiet. Then we sneaked out and saw that Aunt Sophie was still breathing. We carried her inside the barn and then went looking for others who might have survived the brutal attack by the Indians. Everyone was dead. Scalped," she sniffled, the tears rolling down her cheeks. "Papa and my poor little brother, Tommy. He was only fourteen years old. Uncle John was dead, too. He was Aunt Sophie's husband. She was married to my father's brother."

"I'm truly sorry," Bolt said softly. "It must have been a terrible thing for you women to see."

"It was," Veronica said sadly. "There were others dead. The hired hands and the family who helped us. Mama and I hitched up the wagon as fast as we could and got Aunt Sophie loaded in. We got away just in time because two of those Indians came back and torched the barn and the other buildings. They're the ones who've been chasing us."

"I know you must have been frightened," Bolt said, "but you got away from the Indians and that's what important."

"I sent Mama on ahead with the wagon and I rode through the village, hoping to find some survivors." Veronica shook her head. "I couldn't find anyone. Everyone was dead. Everyone was burned out. I've never known such sadness as when I rode away from our village and saw all the smoldering fires. I wanted to go looking for Heather, but I knew that those brutal Comanche warriors would . . . would use her and then kill her like they did all the others."

"Maybe she's still alive," Bolt offered in the way of comfort.

"My poor little sister," Veronica said, shaking her head. "Heather just turned eighteen last month and she was to have been married in June. Her fiance, Larry Franklin, was one of those killed by the Indians. I'm glad Heather never knew about Larry's brutal death." Veronica's shoulders shook with quiet sobs as she buried her face in her hands. After a minute, she raised her head and wiped away the tears. "Mama mustn't see me like this."

"Why?" Bolt asked. "She knows you're grieving, same as she is, I'm sure."

"Yes, but Mama keeps her grief inside herself. I've tried, but it all just came pouring out when I started talking to you. Please forgive me."

"Sometimes it's better to let it out, talk about it," Bolt said. "You keep it inside too long and it'll start festering."

Veronica looked over at him, her dark eyes softer. "Sometimes I wish I had died with the others. The grief is almost more than I can bear."

Bolt wanted to hold her in his arms and give her the comfort she needed. "Sharing your grief with someone else helps to ease the pain some."

"Maybe so," she sighed.

"Time will help, too."

Veronica turned and looked over her shoulder as the wagon rumbled up behind her and rolled to a creaking stop. "We were the only three who got away," she said. "That's Mama up there driving the wagon. Aunt Sophie's inside."

Bolt turned and nodded to the older woman who sat atop the hard wagon seat. He saw that she, too, looked dazed and haggard. Her black, rumpled dress was spattered with trail dirt and the fancy black hat she wore looked tattered and it had been crushed into an odd shape.

"Are you all right, Mama?" Veronica asked.

"Yes," her mother said, her voice weak and hoarse. "I hope Sophie's still alive."

"I'm sure she is, Mama. She's got a strong heart and the will to live."

"I'll check on her," Bolt told Veronica in a low voice. He strolled over to the back of the wagon and lifted the flap.

The woman inside was stretched out on the floor of the buggy, two blankets under her and another one, spotted with blood stains, spread across her still body and snugged up to her neck. The woman's head was at the far end of the buggy and the only thing Bolt could see of her was the pale, sallow mask of her face and the tangled mass of light brown hair that flared out around her face on the blood-stained pillow that was propped under her head. He guessed her to be about the same age as Veronica's mother.

He watched the blanket long enough to see it rise and fall with her shallow breathing.

Tom walked up beside Bolt and peered inside. He backed away and shook his head. "Is she still alive?" he whispered.

"Just barely, I'd say. She looks pretty bad, doesn't she?" Bolt spoke in a low voice.

The woman's eyelids fluttered open, then drooped shut again. Again Bolt watched her blanket until he saw it move with her breathing. He stepped back and let the canvas flap back down.

"She needs a doctor, but she shouldn't be riding in that wagon any more," Tom said, still whispering. "I don't think she'd survive the trip to town."

"I don't either." Bolt glanced over at his friend and gave him a puzzled look. "You ain't going soft-hearted on me, are you, Tom?" he grinned.

"Not me," Tom said as the two men walked around to the front of the wagon.

"Is she . . . ?" Veronica said.

"She's still alive," Bolt said.

"Will you please help us, mister?" Veronica pleaded, a look of desperation in her eyes.

"My name's Bolt. Jared Bolt. And this here's my friend, Tom Penrod."

The girl gave each of them a quick nod. "Please, sirs, we need your help," she begged as she twisted the reins in nervous hands. "We've been riding for days and we need to rest for a spell. Aunt Sophie's doin' poorly and Mama and I are so tired we can't go on. We just need a place to sleep tonight where the Indians can't find us. We'll be gone by first light of day, I promise. Oh, please."

"I think we can put you up for the night," Bolt said with an easy smile. "How long has it been since you've eaten?"

Veronica lowered her head and stared down at her hands. "A couple of days, I guess," she said softly. "We found some berries yesterday morning."

"We'll see that you get a proper meal."

"Oh, we'd be most grateful, sir. I . . . we can't thank you enough for your kindness."

"No need to," Bolt said. "Just ride on over to that big log cabin over yonder. Take the wagon over there and we'll help you get your aunt inside. Maybe after a couple of days of rest, she'll be fit to travel again."

Tom frowned at Bolt.

"I don't know how to thank you. We've got no money," Veronica said.

"We wouldn't take it if you had it," Bolt said. "I'm sure you'd do the same for us."

"You two gentlemen are truly kind and we are most grateful for your help." She snapped the reins and motioned for her mother to follow with the wagon.

"A couple of days?" Tom whispered harshly as he and Bolt strolled across the yard toward the bordello after the women were gone. "I thought you were gonna put 'em up just for the night."

"That old woman can't travel in her condition, Tom, and the girls won't be back for a couple of days, so we've got plenty of room."

"Yeah, and I suppose you'll have me washing dishes for the whole lot of them," Tom muttered as he kicked at the grass beneath his feet.

"Not a bad idea," Bolt grinned.

"I told you you'd get involved," Tom sulked.

"I ain't involved, Tom. I'm merely offering shelter to three weary travelers. Folks have done the same for us in the past."

"Yeah, but I know you, Bolt. And with our

luck, those three weary travelers will probably draw those goddamn murdering Indians right to our doorstep."

CHAPTER THREE

Linda Ramsey was already standing on the long wooden porch of the bordello by the time Bolt and Tom strolled across the yard and walked up to the covered wagon. She smiled down at the new arrivals with a look of anticipation and if she was curious about them, it didn't show on her face.

Linda looked as innocent as a blushing bride, and nothing like the scantily-clad, painted harlot she became at night, during working hours. Her face was freshly scrubbed, her long blond hair brushed to a sheen. She wore a plain blue gingham frock, long-skirted, and even though the front of the dress buttoned clear up to her neck, it couldn't hide the voluptuous curves of her large bosom and her slender waist.

Veronica Morningstar still sat her horse and her mother remained on the high seat of the covered wagon, which was right in front of the steps to the log house. Some thirty yards behind them were the two long hitchrails that would be lined with the horses of eager customers if the bordello were open for business right then.

"Linda, we've got guests for the night," Bolt called up to the pretty young blonde.

Linda smiled warmly as she glanced at both women. "Good. I'll be glad for the company."

"Linda, this is Veronica Morningstar," Bolt said as he strolled up to Veronica's horse. "And that's her mother over there. Two weary travelers."

"Hi," Linda beamed.

"Mama's name is Bertha. Bertha Morningstar," Veronica said, her voice still husky from weakness and thirst. She licked her dry lips.

Bolt reached up and helped Veronica slide down from the saddle. As he caught the young woman in his arms and lowered her until her feet touched the ground, he was stunned to feel how light and thin her body actually was. He held her around the waist until she was steady on her feet.

"Are you all right?" he asked as he looked into her dark, sad eyes.

"A little weak and shaky, but I'll be fine," she said, a thin smile on her lips.

"That's Linda Ramsey up there," Bolt announced in a louder voice. "She'll see that you're comfortable."

"Pleased to meet you both," Linda said as she came around the porch railing and bounced down the steps. "I hope you're hungry. I'm fixing chicken and dumplings for supper."

"These women are literally starving to death, Linda," Bolt said seriously. "Their village was attacked by Indians and they've been riding for several days with little food and water."

"Oh, how terrible," Linda said as she looked at the haggard, distraught girl who was about her age. "I hope neither of you were hurt."

"Veronica's aunt was wounded," Bolt said. "She's in the back of the wagon and she's pretty sick. These three women were the only ones to survive the Comanche attack. They lost the rest of their family members and many of their friends."

"Oh, I'm so sorry to hear that," Linda said. "Please come in and I'll fix you some chicken broth and biscuits right away, and then you can rest."

Bertha Morningstar scooted across the wagon seat and Tom rushed over to help her down.

"Thank you. I'll be fine now, young man," Bertha said when she was on the ground. "If you and your friend could help us get Sophie inside, I'd be grateful."

"Don't worry about it, Mrs. Morningstar," Tom said. "We'll carry Sophie into the house. Can you make it up those steps?"

"Yes, thank you," the older woman said firmly. "I'm a pretty tough old bird."

"Can I carry your bags for you?" Linda offered.

"We don't have anything except the clothes on our backs," Veronica said, her voice cracking as she struggled to keep her emotions in check. "We lost everything we owned when those ... those brutal Indians burned our village to the ground."

"I'm truly sorry," Linda said. "It must have

been a terrible ordeal for you."

"It was," Veronica said, her voice no more than a sad whisper.

The older woman tugged at the matted strands of dark, graying hair around her neckline, as if to comb them with her hand. Her face drawn taut, her lips cracked from dryness, Bertha stood tall and rigid beside the covered wagon. "We Morningstars come from strong stock," she said proudly. "We will not sit around and be overcome by grief, nor will we indulge in self-pity. We accept the tragedies that come our way, as well as the blessings, because we know that these things are God's will."

"I think the good Lord allows for grieving," Bolt said quietly.

"We must be strong. We must go on," Mrs. Morningstar said, her words flat and empty of feeling. She turned and made her way to the back of the wagon.

Bolt wondered if Bertha was trying to convince herself of her own strength, of her own faith. He watched her and saw a woman tired beyond her own endurance, a woman older than her years, a woman about to crack right down the middle if she didn't allow herself some flexibility in her staunchness.

"Please come inside and I'll fix you something to eat," Linda said. "You all must be terribly weak and hungry." She started up the steps, then turned to offer her assistance.

Veronica followed Linda up the stairs. She refused Linda's help, but in her frail condition, she clutched the railing for support. Bolt turned and walked to the back of the wagon where Bertha was instructing Tom to be careful with the injured woman.

"Just slide her out easy," Bertha said to Tom, who was inside the wagon. She held the flap open and peered inside.

Bolt reached over and gently pulled on the blankets that were under the wounded woman, tugging her across the floor of the covered wagon toward the entrance as Tom slowly scooted the injured woman forward from inside. The woman, still covered with a blanket that was snugged up around her neck, flinched slightly at the movement. When the afternoon light struck her ashen face and the tangled mass of her blood-matted hair, her eyes fluttered open, then closed again.

Tom hopped down from the wagon, turned and slipped one hand and arm under the woman's bruised back.

"Be careful of her left shoulder," Bertha cautioned as she hovered over the proceedings. "Sophie's got a bad gash there."

Tom nodded and slid his other hand under Sophie's knees, lifted her up in his arms, keeping the blankets in place.

"Let me help you, Tom," Bolt said.

"I've got her. She's as light as a feather." With no effort, Tom carried her around to the front of the wagon and up the steps where Linda and Veronica waited for them on the porch of the log cabin bordello.

"You be careful of her now," Bertha called to

Tom as she walked slowly to the stairway.

Bolt offered Mrs. Morningstar his arm, but she stubbornly refused it.

"I can make it on my own, young man," the older woman said as she reached for the hand rail at the bottom of the steps and pulled herself up to the first step.

Bolt saw how unsteady the woman was on her feet as she took the steps one at a time. "I'm sure you can," he said as he followed right behind her in case she slipped.

Bertha paused halfway up the short flight of stairs and glanced over her shoulder. "We're grateful for your hospitality, young man," she said, puffing for air.

Bolt knew she had stopped to catch her breath, but when he again reached up to help her, she turned and pulled herself up another step. Stubborn old bat, he thought.

"We're glad we can help you, ma'am." He kept his hands out in front of him, prepared to catch Mrs. Morningstar if she faltered.

The others had just entered the house and Linda stood in the doorway, holding the door open for Mrs. Morningstar, as Bertha reached the top of the steps. Above the open door was a wooden sign proclaiming the house to be the ROCKING BAR BORDELLO. Bertha didn't look up. She paused again once she was on the porch, her hand lingering on the railing for support.

"I want you to know we don't take charity, mister," she said as Bolt came up beside her. "Lord knows we don't have any money right now,

36

but somehow we'll pay you back for the night's food and lodging."

"No need to, ma'am," Bolt said as he took her by the arm and escorted her across the threshold and into the parlor of the big log house.

"We live a good Christian life, young man," Bertha said with a proud nod of her head as she pulled her arm away Bolt's grip. "We don't leave any debts unpaid. As soon as we regain our strength, we'll scrub your floors or do your laundry, or something, to pay our way."

"Help thy neighbor," Bolt said. "That's all we're doin', ma'am. Same as you'd do for someone else who needed your help."

"Please sit down on one of the sofas over there, ladies," Linda said. "I'll get you some chicken broth right away." She gestured across the long parlor toward the groupings of the two plush sofas and several overstuffed chairs, the low, sturdy tables that were made of heavy oak.

"I need to take care of Sophie first," Bertha said.

"The first thing you need to do is get your own strength back, Mrs. Morningstar," Bolt said. "Please sit down."

"I don't care about myself," Bertha said. "I've got to tend to Sophie. She's my responsibility." She took a couple of steps toward Tom and Sophie, then faltered. She reached for the back of a straight back chair and regained her balance before Bolt could get to her.

Bolt could see that the older woman was about to collapse from exhaustion. "Mrs. Morningstar, if you don't take care of yourself, you won't be any good to Sophie or anyone else. We'll take care of Sophie for you, so don't you worry about it."

"Hummph," she snorted. "I doubt that you're capable of giving poor Sophie the kind of care she needs."

"We've mended a few broken bodies in our time, Mrs. Morningstar."

"What's that supposed to mean?" she snapped.

"Nothing. People get hurt. We take care of them. Please sit down, both of you."

As the two women strolled obediently to the soft sofas, they had their backs to the other side of the large room where a lavish bar stretched across the far wall. The upright piano sat idle in one corner of the room near the bar, as did the small stage just beyond the piano.

During the daytime, and on Sunday evenings when the bordello was always closed, the massive parlor served as a quiet sitting room for the girls who lived there. On most evenings, however, except for this time when the other harlots were on holiday and the bordello was closed for business, the parlor became a loud, boisterous gathering place for the many customers who came there to be pleasured.

Bolt smiled as he watched the way Mrs. Morningstar sat properly, rigidly, on one of the sofas. He was glad these women had wandered in off the trail at a time when the bordello was closed, the harlots gone, except for Linda. He thought the shock of discovering that she was staying in a house of pleasure would probably kill poor old Bertha.

"Where do you want me to put Sophie? Upstairs?" Tom asked from across the room where he stood with the limp body of the wounded woman in his arms. He leaned against the polished bannister at the bottom of the stairway that went to the upstairs bedrooms.

"Better put her back here in Harmony's room for now," Linda said as she walked past Tom, heading for the kitchen in the back of the house.

Bolt followed Tom down the hall and into Harmony's room, which was decorated in soft, feminine pinks and purples. As the young madam of the whorehouse, and friend to all of the harlots, Harmony spent most of her nights sleeping in this downstairs bedroom. Often on Sunday nights, she slept in Bolt's bed. Even though Harmony had been gone nearly a week now, her delicate scent lingered in the room.

Bolt pulled the bed covers back and Tom placed Sophie gently on the bed.

"She"s a strong-willed, stubborn old mule, ain't she?" Tom said as he walked across the room and dipped a washcloth into the bowl of water that sat on the dresser.

"Who? Bertha?" Bolt chuckled as Tom came back to the bed and began to dab at Sophie's blood-caked face with the damp cloth.

"Yeah. She's got spunk. After all she's been through."

"That woman's gonna break apart."

"Why do you say that, Bolt?" Tom glanced up

39

at his friend. "I see Bertha Morningstar as strong and brave. And obviously, she's still got her faith, even though she's lost almost everything to the Indians."

Bolt shook his head. "She's just going through the motions."

"Maybe so."

Sophie didn't wake up or move as Tom leaned over and washed the dried blood from her cheeks and neck.

Bolt walked over and took a clean towel from the stack on a shelf. He carried it back to the bed.

"You know what I think?" he said.

"What?" Tom took the towel and started drying Sophie's face.

"I think Bertha's having a lot of guilt because she didn't try to save her own daughter, Heather, from the Indians. Not her fault. She was in shock after seeing her husband and son killed. But Sophie here tried to rescue Heather and she nearly got killed in her efforts. That's a pretty heavy burden for a woman like Bertha to carry and I'm sure it's worked on her mind these past few days while they've been riding around, lost, on the wild plains of Texas."

"Look here at Sophie," Tom said, ignoring Bolt's comments.

"What is it?" Bolt leaned closer.

"She ain't no old woman like Bertha. She couldn't be more than twenty or so."

"I'll be damned," Bolt said as he looked at the unconscious woman's face. "She is young."

"Didn't Veronica say Sophie was her aunt?"

"Yeah. I guess Veronica's got a very young aunt. We'd better check that tomahawk wound."

Bolt pulled the blanket back and saw the white, blood-stained bandage that looked like it might have been fashioned from a lace-bordered petticoat. The cloth was wrapped around the young woman's shoulder and under her arm and the crimson stain was on the back of her shoulder. Part of her blouse and her left sleeve had been cut away and a small area of her firm, young breast was exposed.

Tom leaned forward and watched as Bolt gently peeled the outer layer of cloth away. He saw that the wound had been tightly packed with more layers of white cloth.

"Looks like the bleeding has stopped," he said.

"I think so," Bolt agreed. He started to remove the cloth packing, then put it back in place.

"Think we should change the dressing now?" Tom asked.

"No. It's packed pretty good," Bolt said as he snugged the outer bandage back around the wound. "Let's wait a little while. This poor woman's been bouncing around in the back of that wagon for days and I think she needs to just rest right now."

"Think she'll be all right?"

"She's made it this far. If we can bring her out of this deep sleep she's in, I think she'll be all right."

"Sophie's pretty, isn't she?" Tom said as he stared down into the girl's face.

41

"I hadn't noticed, but yes, she is."

Bolt pulled the blanket up around Sophie's neck and the two men turned and walked out of the room. As they headed back toward the parlor, they heard the voices of the three women in the parlor.

"Your last name is Ramsey?" Veronica asked.

"Yes," Linda responded.

"Then you're not married to either one of those fellows?"

"Who? Tom or Bolt? No," Linda giggled. "I'm not married to anyone. I live down here in this . . . this log cabin and Bolt and Tom live in the big ranch house up on the hill."

"Then this is your house," Veronica said.

"No," Linda said. "Bolt and Tom own it. It's part of their ranch, but I consider it my home."

"Interesting, but I don't understand it," Veronica said. "Is Mr. Bolt married?"

Bolt paused in the doorway and Tom stopped beside him.

"No. Neither one of them are married," Linda said.

"Hmmm. I'm surprised some pretty young thing hasn't latched on to Mr. Bolt," Veronica said. "He's quite handsome, I think, in a rugged sort of way. Both men seem very respectable."

Tom nudged Bolt in the ribs with his elbow. "Didn't I tell you?" he whispered, a big grin on his face. "That gal's got her eyes on you, and you're about to become deeply involved. Just like I said you would when they rode up."

"Bullshit," Bolt whispered. "She ain't my type."

"Why not?"
"She asks too damned many questions."

CHAPTER FOUR

"They're both decent fellows," Linda said in response to Veronica's observation of Bolt and Tom. "And personally, I think Tom's a real charmer."

Tom nudged Bolt again. "You hear that?" he whispered.

"Hell, what do you expect her to say?" Bolt said in a hushed voice. "You're keeping her happy in bed. I assume you do it in the dark and she can't see your ugly puss."

"How come you're not married?" Veronica asked Linda. "You're pretty enough."

"I don't know," Linda said. "I guess I haven't found the right fellow yet."

"You like Tom Penrod, don't you? And you say he's a decent young man."

"Yes, but Tom's as hard to catch as a greased pig," Linda giggled. "How's the broth?"

"Good," Veronica said. "It feels good to get something in my stomach."

"How are you doing, Mrs. Morningstar? Do

you want more broth?"

"No thank you. I'm just fine, young lady," Bertha said. "Bless you for the broth. I feel stronger already and with a little sleep, I'll be as good as new."

Bolt and Tom waited a few more minutes before they entered the parlor.

Bertha glanced over at them when they came into the room. She leaned forward and set the empty broth bowl on the low table beside the sofa. "How's Sophie?" she asked, a look of apprehension on her haggard face.

"She's still sleeping," Tom said. "You just stay put and we'll keep a careful watch over her until she wakes up."

"I'll sleep a little while if you don't mind watching over her and then I'll have to sit up all night with her."

"No, you won't," Linda said. "One of us will stay with Sophie through the night. You catch up on your sleep."

"I'll stay with her," Tom said. "I'm going to find some cloth so we can change her dressing in a little while."

"There are some clean flour sacks in the pantry," Linda said.

"Good. I'll get them," Tom said. "Sophie's real young, isn't she?" He glanced across the room at the two women.

Bertha was the one to answer. "Twenty-one last December," she said. "She married my husband's younger brother John, just ten days ago. What a handsome man young Johnnie was. And what a loving couple they were. They had their whole lives ahead of them." She shook her head sadly. "And now John's gone, along with my Cleland and my little Tommy. What a dreadful sight it was to . . ." Bertha cut off her words in the middle of the sentence and swallowed hard.

Bolt could see that she was struggling to keep her emotions in check and he knew that she was remembering the bloody scene of the grotesque murders. He also knew that she was trying to be brave beyond what any human could expect of her.

"Mama, why don't you just let it out?" Veronica cried out in a sudden burst of hysteria. "Go ahead and cry! You must be torn apart inside, just like I am. Show some feeling, damnit!"

Bolt saw Veronica batting back the tears that welled up in her eyes.

"Veronica. I'm shocked at your foul language," Bertha said.

"I'm sorry, Mama. It's just that you're so brave about everything and I'm so weak."

"Don't think that way, Veronica," Bolt said as he walked over to the sofa. "You've both been under a great strain and you have different ways of showing your feelings. Nothing wrong with a good cry."

"Of course I'm saddled by the fateful events that have occurred," Bertha said. "But I won't indulge in self-pity. I was thinking of Sophie. I'm old and I can face such tragedies. But your poor Aunt Sophie." She shook her head again. "She was married and widowed, all in the same week.

Even if her wounds heal, I'm not sure she can survive her grief."

"I'll go back and stay with her," Tom said as he headed for the pantry to pick up the clean cloth.

"You've done a good job of tending to Sophie's wounds, Mrs. Morningstar," Bolt said. "And when she gets better, I'm sure you'll help her through her grief."

"God willing, she'll live." Bertha sighed and stared down at the braided rug between the two sofas, her hands clasped together in her lap.

Veronica sat on the sofa across from her mother. She spooned the last of the broth into her mouth, wiped her mouth with the linen napkin Linda had given her, then set the empty bowl on the low oak table between the two velvet-covered couches.

"Mama," she said, after an awkward pause. "Do you think maybe, by some miracle, that Heather is still alive?"

"Hush, Veronica," her mother said sternly. "We both know very well that those wicked Indians who stole Heather away from us had their way with her. They violated her body, and then murdured her in cold blood, just like they killed and scalped the rest of our good family."

Veronica cringed at her mother's words and looked close to tears again. "But, Mama, there's a chance that Heather's still alive. I want to go out looking for her."

"Veronica, don't speak of such things," Bertha said coldly. "Use your head. Heather is dead. It was God's will."

"But, Mama, how could God be so good and yet be so cruel as to let Heather die like that?"

"Hush, daughter. You must learn to accept God's will, not question it."

Anger flared in Veronica's eyes, but instead of arguing with her mother, she calmed herself and looked directly up at Bolt.

"What do you do for a living, Mr. Bolt?" she asked. "If you don't mind my frankness?"

"I don't mind," Bolt smiled easily, "but please call me just Bolt. Tom and I run a cattle ranch here. The Rocking Bar Ranch. I told you when you first rode up, but you were probably too dazed to remember. Do you feel better now?"

"Yes, the broth helped. Thank you. And I do remember seeing the cattle out there."

"You and your mother should get some rest. Linda will show you to your rooms."

Veronica didn't budge from her spot on the sofa. "You must do a lot of entertaining here," she commented as she glanced around the room. She stared at the bar on the other side of the parlor, and at the shelves behind the polished bartop that held dozens of bottles of expensive whiskey and brandy, and enough sparkling crystal goblets to serve fifty people.

"We do our share of it, I reckon. Would you like a drink?"

"God forbid," Bertha said.

"No thank you," Veronica said politely. "Mama says drinking alcohol is evil."

"It's caused the downfall of many a man," Bertha said. "And it's unthinkable for a lady to even think about tasting the vile poison. I'm surprised you offered it to my daughter."

"Sorry, ma'am," Bolt said, trying to keep the sarcasm from showing. "Where I come from, it's not considered sinful for a lady to have an occasional sip of wine or brandy. And it's often used for medicinal purposes, which is what I intended. I thought a sip or two of brandy would help Veronica relax. As you can see, she's overwrought with grief."

"Well, please don't offer it to her again," Bertha ordered. "I don't want you corrupting her during our short stay with you."

"I had no intention of doing that, ma'am," Bolt said, "but I'll respect your wishes."

"See that you do, young man," Bertha said as she leaned back.

Bolt's temper flared. How dare this woman come into his house and tell him what to do.

Veronica quickly changed the subject. "I understand you're not married, Bolt."

"Nope." Bolt walked a few feet away from the sofa, then turned around and smiled at Veronica. "I can see Linda's been telling tales while we were gone. I hope she didn't tell you everything."

Linda put her hands on her hips. "I was just assuring these nice ladies that you and Tom were decent and respectable. I didn't tell them the bad things," she said with a teasing smile.

"I'd like to hear about that," Veronica said. "It's too bad you don't have a lovely wife to stand by your side when you entertain your guests, but I suppose Linda helps you out when you have parties."

Bolt noticed the odd look Veronica gave Linda, but he wasn't vain enough to think that it was a look of jealousy.

"Oh, yes. Linda's a real big help around here, and my guests always seem to appreciate her many special talents."

"Talents?" Veronica asked. "You mean like cooking fancy food for your guests?"

"You'll have to ask Linda about that," Bolt said. He didn't dare look directly at Linda, but out of the corner of his eye, he could see that she was staring daggers at him. Served her right.

"And what about Harmony?" Veronica prodded. "I assume that if Sophie's using her room, Harmony must live here, too."

"That's right."

"Who is Harmony? Is she your sister, or your aunt? Your mother? A friend?"

"A friend." Bolt said simply. "My mother's been dead for many years."

Bertha perked up. "Then you know what I'm talking about when I say you have to accept the death of a loved one as an act of God."

"I was only a baby when my mother died, Mrs. Morningstar. I don't even remember her, except what my father has told me about her." Bolt was annoyed by Bertha's righteous attitude.

"What about your father? Is he still alive?" Mrs. Morningstar asked.

"Yes, far as I know."

"Is he a cattle rancher, like you?" Bertha said, looking him over.

"Nope. As a matter of fact, my father's a preacher."

"A preacher?" Bertha raised her head and looked over her nose at him, studying him more carefully. "Well, if your father's a preacher, then I'm sure you're a good, kindly, trustworthy gentleman," she said, as if her judgment were the final word on his character. She finally leaned back against the soft sofa and began to relax.

Bolt laughed. "From what I've always heard, preachers' kids were usually ornery brats."

"Are you an ornery brat? A naughty little boy?" Veronica said.

Bolt saw the teasing, almost seductive look in her eyes. "I've been called worse," he said.

Veronica shifted positions, sat up taller. "Where's Harmony now?" she asked. "Will she mind Sophie being in her room?"

"Harmony has taken a little trip. A vacation," Bolt smiled. "That broth has certainly made you inquisitive."

"Oh, I'm sorry. I didn't mean to pry into your personal affairs," Veronica said. "I'm just curious about other people. We've lived on our little farm all my life." Her voice caught in her throat as if she'd suddenly remembered that her farm was gone now.

"Being a curious person myself, I can understand," Bolt said.

Veronica turned and looked up at Linda. "What do you do here, Linda? Are you the maid? The cook?"

Bertha Morningstar suddenly sat up straight,

51

rousing from her dozing position. "You aren't a slave, are you, girl?" She eyed Bolt suspiciously.

"No, I'm not a slave," Linda laughed. "I live here on this ranch because I like it here."

"But what do you do here?" Veronica persisted.

"I work here," Linda said with a smile, "doing what has to be done." She glanced over at Bolt with a playful twinkle in her eyes.

Bolt cleared his throat. "Veronica, I think you're so punchy now, you're just babbling. It's time for you to go upstairs and get some rest. Both you and your mother." He walked over and took the young girl's hand, pulled her to her feet.

"I think the young man's right, Veronica," said her mother as she rose to her feet. "You're just talking nonsense and I've reached the point where I can't think straight anymore. I'll have to trust Sophie's care to your hands."

"Don't worry about her, Mrs. Morningstar. She'll be all right."

"I think I'll just sleep down here on the floor," Veronica said.

"You'll do no such of a thing," Bolt said firmly. "Not when we've got all those empty beds upstairs. Come on, young lady."

"But just look at me. I can't sleep in someone else's bed with these filthy clothes on," she protested. "And I haven't got anything else to wear."

"I'm sure Linda can find some sleeping gowns for both of you ladies. And I'll heat some water so you can take a bath if you want to," Bolt offered. "In fact, I've already got water heating outside. Tom and I were washing the dishes

52

when you rode up."

"Really? I've never heard of men doing dishes before."

"You're got a lot to learn, young lady. Would you like to take a bath before you go to bed? It might help relax you."

"I would be most grateful if I could soak in a tub of hot water for a few minutes," Veronica said.

"I'd like to take a bath, too," Bertha said. "If it wouldn't be too much trouble."

"No trouble at all, ma'am."

"You take yours first, Mama," Veronica offered.

"Bolt," Linda said, "if you'll just fetch the hot water and pour it into the tub, I'll take care of these two ladies. I know you've got chores to do before supper."

"Yes, I do. Chet and Rusty should be back from town by now. If they are, I'll have them take care of the Morningstars' horses and wagon."

"Oh, my, I'd forgotten all about our horses," Bertha said.

"They'll be fed and watered," Bolt assured the older woman.

"Who are Chet and Rusty?" Veronica asked.

"The cowhands," Bolt said. "You ask too many questions, young lady."

"That's what Mama tells me," Veronica said with a slight little laugh. "She says that it's rude and that if I ask too many questions, I might just find out something I'd be better off not knowing."

"That's true, Veronica," Bertha said. "Some things are better left alone."

"Your mother's a wise woman. Better listen to her," Bolt said as he smiled at Bertha.

"Supper will be ready in about two hours, Bolt," Linda said. "As soon as I get these ladies settled in for a nap, I'll cook the vegetables and make the dumplings."

"I'll be here," he said.

Bolt went out to fetch the hot water, glad that he could take it in the back door of the bordello, where the wooden tub was located in a bath room. He didn't care to parry any more of Veronica's curious questions right then. Not that he really cared if the women knew that he ran a bordello, but in their distraught, weakened condition, it would serve no purpose to tell them.

Hopefully, the Morningstars would be gone by the time the harlots returned to the ranch the day after tomorrow. And if the women were still there, they would learn soon enough that they were staying in a house of pleasure.

A feeling of uneasiness settled in Bolt's gut as he walked across the ankle-deep grass. A feeling of apprehension that he couldn't seem to shake.

Tom had been right, he thought, as he realized that he was getting much more involved with these ladies than he'd planned to when he'd offered them food and shelter for a day or two. Now he knew that the Morningstars would be house guests until Sophie recovered enough to move on. That could be days. Or weeks.

And then what would the three women do?

They had no money, no food, no clothes or personal belongings. No place to go.

He knew one thing for certain. He couldn't offer them jobs in his bordello to get them by until they were able to fend for themselves.

He shook his head and smiled. Not to worry, he mused. Things always had a way of working themselves out. Either the women would get so mad they'd ride off in a huff. Or, possibly, they'd get angry enough to burn his house of sin to the ground.

"Damnation! Destroy the evil!" He could see Bertha Morningstar shouting it now, as she put a torch to the Rocking Bar Bordello.

CHAPTER FIVE

Veronica Morningstar yawned as she strolled into the kitchen. Her long, dark hair glistened like a crow's wing as she walked. The kerosene lantern that hung from the middle of the ceiling was lit and she didn't know whether it was morning or night.

Veronica was taller than most girls. Even so, the royal blue, velvet robe she wore reached clear down to her ankles, exposing only her bare feet. Beneath the robe, she wore a sheer sleeping gown that fit her as if it was made for her. She wondered whose clothes she was wearing. They weren't Linda's, she knew, even though Linda had provided her with both garments. Linda was five or six inches shorter than she was.

Before she had taken a nap, Veronica had brushed all of the tangles out of her matted hair, then washed the long, dusty strands as she soaked in the same tub water her mother had used. After the leisurely bath, she had brushed her hair again until it shone.

When she awoke, she riffled through the clothes that hung in a curtained closet in the room where she slept, searching for something to wear. She saw some fancy dresses that she really wanted to try on, and even pulled a couple of them out and held them up to her. But she decided she should ask Linda first. She did, however, indulge in one small pleasure. She opened the bottle of perfume she found on the dresser, smelled it, and then dabbed some of it behind her ears and on her long, graceful neck.

Linda stood at the kitchen counter, her back to Veronica. She was up to her elbows in biscuit batter, kneading the sticky dough for the dumplings she would drop on the boiling stew of chicken chunks and carrots that were freshly picked from the garden.

"Good morning," Veronica said, "although I guess it's really almost night time. I don't know if this is today or tomorrow."

Linda turned the upper part of her body around to look at Veronica, keeping her flour-sticky hands over the dough. "It's still the same day," she laughed. "I guess you finally got some sleep."

"Yes," Veronica said, "but I'm so confused, I don't know whether it's day or night, or even what day it is. I feel like I've slept for two days." She walked over to the counter as Linda turned back to the dumpling dough.

"It's still Wednesday. It's getting dark outside, and you only slept for about an hour," Linda said with a smile as she glanced over at Veronica.

"You needed the rest so badly, I was hoping you would sleep straight through the night. Even so, you look a lot more rested than you did when you first climbed down off your horse four hours ago."

"I feel a lot better. Oh, did you bake a pie?" Veronica asked when she spotted the pie on another part of the long counter.

"I made two of them. This morning, before you got here," Linda said. "Apple pies. I already gave one of them to Chet and Rusty when they got back from town a little while ago."

Veronica walked over and smelled the pie. "Will they be eating supper with us?" she asked casually.

"No. They do their own cooking over at the bunkhouse where they live. But whenever I bake desserts, pies or cookies, or cake, I always fix extra for them. Same as I do for Bolt and Tom. Men like sweets but quite frankly, they're very awkward when it comes to making them."

"Don't Bolt and Tom always eat down here with you?" Veronica asked.

"No, they live in the ranch house up the hill. Harmony usually cooks for them when she's here. Sunday nights are different, though," Linda said as she formed small dumplings out of the dough. "That's when Bolt and Tom come down here and we all sit down to a big, family dinner."

"Family? You mean you're related to them in some way?"

"No. Just an expression," Linda laughed. "We just feel like a big, happy family, that's all."

Veronica gave Linda a puzzled look, then strolled over to the back window and looked out at the darkening sky. "Has it really only been four hours since we stumbled onto this ranch, all lost and scared? It seems like it was yesterday when we got here."

"That's because you napped," Linda said as she wiped the dumpling dough from her sticky fingers, then dunked her hands into a bowl of tepid water to wash them. "It's been almost four hours since you arrived. Your poor mother hasn't slept at all. The last time I was in there to check on Sophie, your mother was sitting in the rocker, nodding off. I don't know how she keeps going."

"Mama's stubborn," Veronica snapped.

Linda glanced over at her. "She's troubled, Veronica. She's very worried about your aunt."

"I know she is," Veronica said in a gentler tone. "So am I. Just now when I stopped by the room to see how Aunt Sophie was faring, I wasn't really surprised to see Mama sitting in there with Tom. Mama looks so tired. I wish she'd go to bed."

"Is your aunt still in a deep sleep?"

"Yes. I hope she comes out of it. Do you think she will?"

"I helped Tom change the dressing a while ago and the deep wound seems to be mending," Linda assured the girl. "I think she'll be all right."

Veronica paced nervously across the room. She leaned over the cook stove and sniffed at the aromatic steam escaping the chicken pot.

"Smells good."

"Are you hungry?"

"Yes, I'm starved."

"Do you want something to eat now?" Linda offered.

"No, I'll wait." Veronica walked back over to the window, leaned closer and peered out at the gray, darkening landscape. "What are all those tiny little buildings out back?" she asked.

Linda's heart leaped to her throat and she swallowed hard. She was suddenly uneasy with Veronica's continuous questions. The girl had been asking them every time Linda had talked to her. Innocent questions, probably, born of idle curiosity and a fascination for a culture that was foreign to her, but annoying just the same.

Linda hadn't minded the questions about her own growing-up years and about the beaus she'd had. That was girl talk. And she wouldn't have minded if Veronica had found out that she was a prostitute. But she certainly wasn't going to divulge anything personal about Bolt, or about the bordello. She respected his privacy too much. She didn't know if Bolt had told Veronica about the bordello, but she wasn't going to be the one to mention it. That was Bolt's business.

"Those are guest cottages," she said.

"Cottages?" Veronica said with surprise as she looked closer. "There couldn't be more than one room in any one of them. Are they just sleeping rooms?"

"Yes."

"Oh, you mean that's where you put your party

guests if they stay over?"

"Yes, sometimes," Linda said truthfully. There had been occasions when the cottages had been used for overnight guests.

Veronica turned away from the window and leaned against a counter. "I wish Bolt would have a party while we're here," she said with a wistful look in her eyes. "Do you know that I've never been to a real party in my life? Just the church socials in our little village and they aren't much fun."

"No, I suppose not," Linda said as she lifted the lid of the chicken pot and stirred the contents. The kitchen instantly filled with the fragrant aroma.

"Do you have fun at Bolt's parties?" Veronica strolled by the cook stove and sniffed the air.

Linda hesitated before she answered. "They're mostly work for me."

"Of course," Veronica said with a smile and an understanding nod. "You probably have to prepare all the fancy food for the party, and then see that the guests have a good time when they get here."

Linda whirled around and wiped her hands on her apron. She glanced toward the hallway. "Speaking of food, Bolt should be here any minute. As soon as he gets here, I'll drop the dumplings in the stew. They won't take long to cook."

"Do you need some help?" Veronica offered.

"You can help me set the table," Linda said, relieved that she didn't have to explain her part in Bolt's so-called parties. "The plates are in that

61

cupboard up there and the clean napkins are in that drawer with the silver napkin holders."

"How many people shall I set for?" the tall girl asked as she opened the cupboard and reached up for the plates.

"There'll be five of us." Linda opened another drawer and counted out the silverware, took it to the table in the middle of the big kitchen.

"Sometimes, do you have costume parties here?" Veronica asked as she placed each of the the five plates around the table.

Linda looked up at the inquisitive girl, a puzzled expression on her face. "Why do you ask that?"

Veronica glanced over at Linda. "Oh, I looked in the closet up there in the room where I slept and I saw some frilly, glittery gowns hanging in there." She rolled a white linen napkin up and slid it into one of the silver holders, set it beside a plate. "Then, when I went into that other room to see if Mama was sleeping, I peeked into that closet, too, and I saw some fancy gowns in there, too."

"Do you always look in other people's closets, Veronica?" Without looking at the girl, Linda turned and walked over to a cabinet and withdrew cups and saucers.

"Mercy, no," Veronica said. "That would be rude. I was just looking for something to wear because I didn't know if it was proper for me to come downstairs wearing this robe and sleeping gown."

"Under the circumstances, you're fine."

Veronica worked in silence, stuffing napkins into the napkin rings, setting them in place beside the other plates. "Some of those dresses looked kind of, well, you know, kind of sexy," she said after a couple of minutes. "That's why I thought you might have costume parties."

"Yes, we dress up in fancy clothes when we're entertaining," Linda said as she carried the cups and saucers to the table.

"Mama would never let me wear a gown like one of those. If I ever did, sure as the sun comes up in the morning, she'd say that I was trying to seduce the devil himself."

"After supper I'll find some suitable frocks for you and your mother to wear when you get up in the morning."

"How many women live here?" Veronica asked.

"Six of us. Seven, counting Harmony." Linda walked over to the cook stove and checked the pot of green beans that were simmering.

"I noticed that Harmony's room down here is a little fancier than the upstairs bedrooms? Is Harmony someone special?"

"She is to us," Linda said. "She's like a mother hen to the rest of us. She's a good friend. Someone to talk to."

"Harmony's an older woman, then. Is she a grandmother, or an elderly spinster?"

"Harmony? No," Linda laughed. "She's only a couple of years older than the rest of us girls."

"You mean the other women who live here are young, like yourself?"

"Yes. We range in age from eighteen to twenty-two. I think Harmony is about twenty-four."

"Hmmm. I figured the women who lived here were all different ages. In fact, I thought most of them were elderly widows or older spinsters."

"What made you think that?" Linda reached up in a cupboard and brought down two china serving bowls.

"I just find it hard to imagine girls your age living away from home. Mama says it isn't proper for a young girl to move out of her parents' house until she gets married. She says that vile things can happen to a young, unsuspecting lady who lives away from home."

"Lots of young women live on their own without being violated, Veronica. Some go away to finishing school. Some move to big cities where they can find domestic work. Some teach school and live in boarding houses."

"About a year ago my friend Betsy and I dreamed about taking the stagecoach to St. Louis, but Mama wouldn't let me go. She said it wouldn't be proper for us to be in a big city by ourselves, that people would think us sinful."

"Your mother is just trying to protect you, Veronica. You should be glad she cares about you." Linda set the sugar bowl and the matching pitcher for the cream on the counter, then looked around to see what else needed to be done.

"I am glad she cares," Veronica said. "But she treats me like I was still a little girl. I don't think she's noticed that I'm all grown up now."

"Mothers are like that," Linda smiled. In a way, she felt sorry for Veronica. The immature girl had obviously led a sheltered life under the thumb of her strong, domineering mother. She knew by Veronica's questions that Bolt had not told her about the bordello. As naive as Veronica was, the shock would have been too much for her to bear.

"Is this place a boarding house?" Veronica asked.

"I guess you could call it that."

"Do you pay room and board?" Veronica persisted.

Linda sighed, tired of answering the girl's questions. "No, we don't."

"Does Bolt provide for all of your needs?"

"In a way, I suppose he does." Linda walked away from the tall girl and checked the stew again, wishing Bolt would hurry up so they could get on with supper. "Why don't you pull out a chair and sit down, Veronica? Everything is ready."

Veronica did as she was told, as if she had been ordered to do so by her mother. She sat quietly for a few minutes, watching the blond-headed, large-breasted girl walk across the kitchen floor as Linda gathered up some of the dirty cooking utensils and stacked them on one end of the counter.

"Is Bolt wealthy?" she asked after a short time.

"You ask a lot of questions, Veronica." Linda turned and frowned at the slightly younger woman. "I know nothing about Bolt's financial situation. If you want to know, you'll have to ask him."

"I didn't mean that the way it sounded," Veronica said in way of apology. "I wasn't trying to pry into Bolt's personal affairs and I really don't care to know whether he's got money or not. I was just remembering how hard Papa had to work to keep food on the table for our small family of four. To run a cattle ranch like this, with so many to feed, the cowhands, you girls, the cattle, it must take more money than my father ever dreamed of having. That's all I meant."

Linda felt badly that she had snapped at the girl. She had to remind herself that Veronica had never been outside of her own small village before, and that she was probably experiencing a whole new world that was both confusing and awesome to her.

"I wouldn't say that Bolt was wealthy," Linda said in a gentler tone. "He and Tom are partners and I don't suppose they make any more money than any of the other cattle ranchers around here. I know that there are good times in the cattle business, and there are bad times. Bolt and Tom seem to flow with the tides, same as everybody else."

"But it must cost Bolt a lot of money to support all of you girls," Veronica said. "All those clothes you have."

"We earn our keep," Linda said abruptly.

"How?" Veronica asked. "What do you do around here all day?"

"During the day? Oh, there's plenty to do around the ranch. We girls feed the chickens, gather the eggs, milk the cows when the cowhands are too busy with their own chores. We keep this house spotless. We tend to the garden where we grow most of the food that is eaten by everybody who lives here at the ranch, including Bolt and Tom, Chet and Rusty, and the extra hands Bolt takes on from time to time."

"I didn't realize you did so much around here," Veronica said.

"We do a lot more," Linda said as she washed the dirty cooking utensils and the cutting boards she had used to prepare the evening meal. "During harvest time, we spend days preserving the food so we'll have enough to last us through the winter. Harmony cooks and cleans for Bolt and Tom. She mends their socks and washes their clothes so they're free to take care of the cattle. We help her clean the big ranch house sometimes. And when we've got any spare time during the day, we make our own clothes."

Veronica got up and walked over to the counter. "Where are your tea towels? I'll dry those dishes for you."

"In that drawer." Linda pointed with her elbow because her hands were in the basin of water.

Veronica dried two big knives and set them aside. "Where do you girls get the money to buy the material for those fancy gowns? Does Bolt pay you for working here?"

"Yes, he does."

Veronica's face brightened. "Maybe Bolt would let me work here for a few days. Just until I could earn a little money so Mama and Aunt Sophie and I could ride on to San Antonio. If we had enough money for food and lodging for a couple of days, I know I could find work. Do you think he'd let me work with you girls, Linda?"

Linda cringed at the thought. "I don't know. You'd have to ask him about that." She shook the wash water from her hands, then grabbed a towel and dried them. She walked across the room and peered down the hall.

Veronica picked up the cutting board and dried it. She turned and looked over at Linda. "Have you ever gone to bed with either Bolt or Tom?"

Stunned by the bold question, Linda whirled around and glared at the naively insensitive girl. "That's none of your business, Veronica. You ask too damned many questions."

"I'm sorry," Veronica said quietly. "I guess that was rude of me to ask such a personal question."

"Indeed it was." Linda marched over to the cook stove and lifted the lid of the stew pot.

"I didn't mean anything by it, Linda. I was just thinking out loud."

"Well, please leave me out of your thoughts." Linda reached over and picked up a handful of the raw dumplings and carefully placed them on top of the bubbling broth. "You must be exhausted, Veronica. I think you and your mother need to go to bed soon, so I'm going to go ahead and cook the dumplings. If Bolt isn't here by the time they're done, he can eat later."

Veronica waited until Linda had finished putting all of the dumplings in the broth before she spoke again. "Linda, didn't you ever wonder what it would be like to sleep with a certain man?"

Linda looked at the girl. "Yes. I suppose I have."

"That's all I was doing. Wondering what Bolt would be like in bed."

"I wouldn't know anything about Bolt in bed, Veronica. I've never slept with him." Linda turned away with a dramatic flair. "You'll have to find that out for yourself!"

CHAPTER SIX

The aroma of chicken and dumplings filled the house and assaulted Bolt's nostrils when he entered the front door of the bordello. He had been so busy with the chores, he hadn't realized how hungry he was until just then.

A single glowing lantern bathed the large parlor in a soft, golden light. He glanced around the quiet room and was not surprised to find it empty. He figured that Veronica Morningstar and her mother had retired to separate rooms after their baths and that once they climbed into the soft feather beds, they would sleep through until morning.

He didn't hear any sounds at all when he strolled across the room and into the hall that led to the back of the house. The light from the kitchen spilled into the darkened hall. Before he got to the kitchen, he turned right, into a shorter hallway that went to Harmony's two-room living quarters.

He smelled the strong odor of liniments and balm even before he entered the open door of Harmony's small sitting room. He walked on through the dimly lit room and into the bedroom that was decorated with Harmony's feminine touch. A pink comforter on the bed where Sophie lay, crocheted runners on the tables and dresser, fluffy pink ruffles around the dressing table that held several pretty bottles of perfume, frilly pink curtains at the window, and a matching curtain hanging across the entrance to her closet.

Bertha was asleep in a small overstuffed chair beside the bed, her head drooping to her chest, her hands folded in her lap. Bolt noticed that her hair was clean and brushed, the dirt smudges gone from her face. She wore the same black dress, but most of the dust and caked-on dirt had been either brushed away, or washed clean. Even though she was asleep, her face was lined with fatigue.

Tom stood at the other side of the bed, holding a wet cloth on Sophie's forehead. He glanced up when Bolt walked into the room.

"How is she?" Bolt asked in a hushed voice.

"She's still unconscious," Tom sighed. He removed the compress from Sophie's forehead and set the damp cloth in the basin of water on the table beside the bed. A stack of clean, white bandaging material sat next to the line of medicinal liniments and balms made from herbs.

Bertha raised her head and opened her eyes. "Sophie, is that you?" she mumbled. She came fully awake and looked at each of the men. "Oh, is Sophie awake? I thought I heard her calling me."

Tom shook his head. "No, she's still in a deep sleep."

"Have you checked that tomahawk wound yet?" Bolt asked.

"Yes," Tom said. "Linda and I changed the dressing a while ago. That gash is deep and wicked. It went clear to the bone. The wound seems to be mending, but it's gonna take a long time for the flesh to grow back together."

"It'll heal from the inside out, but we'll have to make sure it doesn't get infected," Bolt said.

"Poor girl is a mass of bruises," Tom said. "Big purple blotches all over her arms and back. And she's got a lump on the back of her head the size of a goose egg."

"The bump on her head is probably what's causing her to be unconscious," Bolt said. He turned to Bertha. "Has Sophie been like this since she got hurt?"

"No, she's rallied around every day," the older woman said as she pushed herself up out of the chair. "She comes and goes."

"That's a good sign. She'll come around."

"Bolt. I didn't know you were back," Linda said as she came into the room. "We've been waiting supper on you. Come on, folks, the food's ready."

"I'll stay with Sophie," Tom said.

"No need to, Tom," Bolt said. "She'll come around when she's ready."

"Young man," said Bertha, "I'm grateful for the care you're giving Sophie but you can leave her side long enough to eat."

"I should stay," Tom said.

"Aw, come on, Tom," Linda begged. "The dumplings will turn doughy if they're not eaten right away."

Tom glanced down at Sophie's pale, pretty face, then turned and joined the others as they walked to the kitchen.

Bolt was surprised to see Veronica standing by the kitchen table, even more stunned by her beauty, which he hadn't really noticed before. "I thought you'd be fast asleep," he said as he gazed into her bright, dark eyes that seemed to sparkle with anticipation.

"I napped," she said, with a smug smile.

"You look, well, you look more rested than when I first saw you," he stammered. "How do you feel?"

He couldn't take his eyes off Veronica. The bright blue robe she wore hung gracefully from her straight shoulders and she looked much taller than what Bolt had remembered as his first impression of the desperate, frazzled girl. Her shiny black hair hung loosely about her face and when she moved her head, the strands glimmered with streaks of gold reflected from the lamp light. Her smooth, clear complexion was without blemish except for a small brown mole high on her left cheek.

"I feel like I'm walking around in a daze, with everything around me not quite real," Veronica laughed. "And yet, I feel like I've slept for days."

"You're about to drop from exhaustion. Both you and your mother," Bolt said.

"I know I'm weak and shaky, but I don't seem to be able to relax enough to sit still for a minute. I don't know whether it's from hunger or lack of sleep."

"Probably both," Bolt said. "You both can get a good night's sleep after you eat and I'm sure you'll wake up in better spirits in the morning. Hopefully, Sophie will wake up feeling better, too."

As Bertha shuffled up to the oblong table, Bolt pulled out the end chair and held it for her. Tom walked over and sat in his usual spot, along the side of the table, at the far end. After Bolt pushed Bertha's chair in, he sat in the empty chair between Tom and Bertha.

"Go ahead and sit down, Veronica," Linda said. "I'll serve the food."

Veronica sat in the chair in front of her, next to her mother and across from Bolt. "I hope you're right, Bolt," she said. "We need to be on our way in the morning."

"Why so soon? Where are you going to go?" Bolt stared across the table at her as she pulled the napkin from its silver ring and placed the linen cloth in her lap.

"I don't know yet," Veronica said sadly. "We'll find a place. We'll survive. We have to."

"We're Morningstars," Bertha added as Linda set the steaming pot of chicken and dumplings in the middle of the table.

"Sophie's in no condition to be moved," Tom said. "You can't leave in the morning."

"You don't have anyplace to go," Linda said. "You can't just keep riding. Rest up tomorrow and maybe we can help you find a place to stay." She set a bowl of seasoned green beans on the table and took her place beside Veronica, across from Tom.

"Linda and Tom are right," Bolt said. "You should stay at least one more day."

"We'll stay the night and no longer," Bertha said firmly. "We are not beggars, Mr. Bolt." She sat straight in the hard chair, her hands in her lap.

"Never mind," Bolt said. "We'll talk about it in the morning when you're both more rested. May I dish you up, Mrs. Morningstar?" He reached for the ladle in the stew pot.

"Haven't you forgotten something, Mr. Bolt?" Bertha said coldly.

"What's that?"

"In our family, we say the blessing before we eat. Being a preacher's son, I would think that you would, too."

Bolt withdrew his hand from the ladle and put both hands in his lap. "Would you be kind enough to give the blessing, Mrs. Morningstar?"

With all heads bowed, Bertha began. "Lord, we thank Thee for this bountiful food we are about to eat. We thank Thee for this shelter Thou has provided for us. Please bless this house and keep it safe from harm or evil. Bless these kind people who have taken us in and given us a safe refuge from our troubles. Please bless Sophie and make her well. Bless those loved ones who have gone on to eternal peace before us. Please show us Thy path to take. Please guide us on our journey. We thank Thee. Amen."

"Amen," the others echoed.

Bertha raised her head, picked up her dinner plate and offered it to Bolt. "Just a small amount, please," she said.

The subject of the women leaving in the morning was never brought up during the meal. Veronica ate a heartier supper than her mother did and asked a lot of general questions about the cattle-raising business. Did Bolt and Tom drive their own cattle to market? Where did they get the cows in the first place? What was it like to sleep out under the stars on the lonely prairie with all those scary, wild animals nearby? Did they brand their cattle, and what did the brand look like? Why did they settle in Cow Town, and did they have to go out in the pasture and count their cattle every day?

As Linda cleared the dirty dishes away and brought clean, smaller plates and the apple pie to the table, Veronica asked if San Antonio would be a good place for the three women to make their home. Following some discussion, she announced that she had decided to become a schoolmarm.

Linda was just about to cut into the pie when they all heard the moan from the nearby room.

Tom was the first one to scramble out of his chair. "That's Sophie," he yelled as his chair legs scraped against the wooden planks of the floor. He dashed toward the sick girl's room and the others followed close behind.

"Heather," Sophie moaned. "Where are you, Heather?" She tossed her head from side to side, made a feeble attempt to sit up.

"It's all right, Sophie," Tom said as he reached her bedside. He gently lowered her head back to the pillow, then felt her forehead with the palm of his hand.

"Who are you? Where am I?" Sophie asked in a dry, husky voice as she tried to focus on the stranger's face above her.

Bolt was the second one to reach Sophie's side. He stared down at her as Linda and Veronica came up behind him. Sophie shuffled up an instant later. She stood back with the girls.

"You're with friends, Sophie. Just relax," Tom said in a soothing voice.

Sophie's eyes fluttered, then closed. Her body went limp.

"She's gone under again, damnit." Tom shook his head. "She's got a fever."

Suddenly Sophie's eyes popped wide open. She tried to get up as she stared up at Tom, a look of terror in her eyes.

"No! No," she cried in a weak voice. "Get away! Get away from me! Run, Heather! Run! Hurry! Get away, you evil, murdering monster!"

"Settle down, Sophie," Tom said as he placed his hand on her good shoulder and kept her down. "You're safe now."

"Run, Heather! Run to the barn!" Sophie cried out. "Get away from me."

The eerie tone of her low, husky voice sent a shiver down Bolt's spine as he stared into her panic-stricken face.

"She's reliving the horror," Veronica said softly. She turned her head away and batted back the tears that streamed freely down her cheeks.

"Come on, Veronica," Linda said. "Let's wait in the kitchen. We can't do anything to help her right now. Let the fellows handle it." She put her arm around the sobbing girl's waist and led her out of the room.

Bolt glanced around. He saw Bertha watching her daughter exit the room. Then the older woman turned her attention back to the delirious girl on the bed. With no emotion showing on her face, Bertha stood back several feet and stared at Sophie.

"Run, Heather! Run to the barn!" Sophie screamed again, the haunting husk still in her voice. "Don't hit me! Run, Heather! Get away or I'll kill you!"

"It's all right, Sophie. Relax," Tom said, still trying to calm the girl.

Sophie struggled to get up and Tom pushed against her good arm, pinning it to the soft bed. Hatred replaced the fear in her eyes as Sophie raised her free arm, as if to strike out. Because of the tomahawk wound to that shoulder, the arm rose only about two inches above the bed before it dropped back down to the pink comforter, totally useless.

"That's a good girl," Tom said in a gentle voice as he eased up on the pressure on her arm. "You're safe now, Sophie. Nobody's gonna hurt you."

Wild-eyed, Sophie looked at him as if she were a sleek, stalking panther studying its prey, waiting for the right moment to attack. "You murderer!" she shouted, her voice somewhat stronger, but nonetheless eerie in its huskiness. "Run, Heather! Faster! Leave me alone or I'll kill you!"

"Please, Sophie," Tom said. "You can trust us. We're your friends. You're safe here."

"You murderer!" she yelled. "Leave Heather alone!" With surprising strength, Sophie jerked her right arm free of Tom's hand. "I'll kill you," she cried as she lashed out at him with her hand. She had no strength behind her thrust and just punched at the empty air. Her arm fell back to the covers, limp after her valiant effort. For a minute, she just lay there and stared up at the heavy, log ceiling beams.

Tom let out a big sigh and glanced over at Bolt, then turned his head and looked back at Bertha, a sheepish grin on his face. "Well, Sophie came up fighting, but at least she's awake."

Bolt watched the older woman. Bertha didn't respond. She just stood there like a black marble statue, cold and hard, her hands clasped together as they rested against her stomach.

"Sophie's been through a shocking ordeal," Bolt said quietly as he turned and looked down at the motionless girl on the bed. "She's out of her mind right now, but I think her reaction is quite normal under the circumstances."

"I do, too, poor girl," Tom agreed. "She must be going through hell."

"She's come out of her deep sleep and that's the important thing," Bolt said. "In time, she'll come to her senses."

Sophie didn't move. Her eyes didn't blink. She just stared up at the ceiling, her mouth slack, spittle dribbling from the corner of her mouth. Although Tom and Linda had made an effort to wash her up, her straw-colored hair was still matted with dirt and dried blood, and as she stared upward with wide, unseeing eyes, she looked like a mangy, rabid animal.

Bolt watched her for a short time and then became concerned. He stepped closer to the bed and leaned over to look into her vacant, pale blue eyes that were like clouded marbles.

Sophie blinked her eyes, then looked up at Bolt's face, which was just inches above her own face. Her forehead knotted to a frown and for a brief instant, she appeared to be studying his rugged features. She blinked again and then her pale eyes seemed to take on color as they flashed with a sudden revulsion. Her mouth twisted up to grotesque shapes as her lips began to twitch and undulate, as if she had developed an uncontrollable tic.

Without warning, Sophie spat in Bolt's face. "You murderer!" she cried.

Bolt jumped back, wiped his face.

"You killed my husband, you foul-smelling bastard," Sophie said, her voice now calmly cold and measured. "You won't get Heather. You can't find Bertha and Veronica. They're hiding. And you won't get me because I'm going to kill you." She bared her teeth like a vicious dog.

"Sophie, you're safe now," Tom said. "We're your friends and Bertha and Veronica are here with us."

Sophie's head jerked as she turned to glare up at Tom, who stood next to Bolt.

"You're dreaming, Sophie," Bolt said tenderly. "It was a nightmare, a bad dream. But it's all over now and you're safe. Please wake up."

Bertha Morningstar suddenly pushed her way between the two men to stand by Sophie's bed.

"Neither one of you know how to take care of this girl," she said as she elbowed them aside. "I knew that from the beginning. You're treating her like she was a baby, but I won't put up with her sassy behavior another minute."

Stunned by Sophie's action, Bolt and Tom stepped back away from the bed. They looked at one another and shrugged their shoulders.

"Stop it right now, girl," Bertha demanded as she took Sophie's wrists and shook them hard. "You're making a fool of yourself, acting this way. Now stop it. You hear me?"

Sophie stared up at Bertha with the same hatred she had shown with the two men. "No, you evil bastard. I'm going to kill you."

"Don't you ever use that kind of foul language in front of me again!" Bertha snarled as she dropped the sick girl's wrists. "You're a Morningstar now, and don't you ever forget it." As if consumed by a sudden, uncontrollable rage, she reached up and pinched Sophie's cheek, shook it hard as she squeezed the soft, tender flesh.

Sophie moaned in pain.

"You ought to be ashamed of yourself, Sophie," Bertha scolded in a harsh voice. "How dare you embarrass me like that in front of these strangers. Now, you grow up and act like a lady. Stop this nonsense right now!" She pinched the cheek harder. "You hear me, girl?"

"No, no. Somebody help me," Sophie cried. "Run, Heather."

Tom rushed up to the bedside and tried to drag the older woman away. "Stop it, Bertha," he shouted. "You're hurting her."

"Leave me alone," Bertha snapped. She elbowed Tom away.

"Let her be," Bolt said as he put his hand on Tom's shoulder and pulled him back.

"But she's crazy," Tom protested.

"Let her be," Bolt said again.

"You listen to me, Sophie Morningstar, and you listen to me good," Bertha said sternly as she continued her verbal assault. She stopped pinching the girl's cheek and took hold of her good shoulder, shook it hard. "I won't tolerate your rude behavior any more, you hear me, Sophie? You've been rambling on like some crazy fool. Feeling sorry for yourself. Acting like a sinful hussy. Spittin' in a man's face. Don't you know it's not ladylike to spit?"

Silent, motionless, the delirious girl stared up at Bertha. Her body was rigid and her eyes flashed with a fire only she understood.

"Are you listening to me, girl?" Bertha yelled. When she got no response, she slapped Sophie across the cheek.

The sound of the blow caused Bolt to wince. Tom's face flushed red with anger. He started to go after Bertha again, but Bolt held him back.

Sophie's facial muscles tautened as her eyes blazed with hatred. She clenched her fingers to a fist and tried to lash out at her attacker.

"Answer me Sophie!" Bertha barked. She slapped the girl again, harder this time.

Sophie's body went limp as she sank deeper into the soft feather bed. Her eyelids drooped shut and she looked like she had before, when she was in the deep sleep of unconsciousness.

Tom shook his head sadly.

Bolt looked at the girl and noticed the tears spilling out of the corner of her eye and rolling down the side of her face. "She's crying, Tom," he whispered.

Sophie opened her eyes, blinked away the tears that blurred her vision. She looked up at the older woman standing over her.

"Bertha?" she asked in a weak voice. "Bertha, is that you?"

"Yes, Sophie. It's me. I'm right here with you," Bertha said in a gentle voice.

"Where am I?" Sophie asked.

"You're in a safe place, thank God," Bertha said as she took Sophie's hand and squeezed it.

Bolt noticed something else as he watched the two women. He noticed the tears that trickled down Bertha's cheeks. He swallowed hard to get rid of the lump that formed in his throat.

"Where's Heather?" Sophie asked as she started to turn her head. "Oh, my head hurts."

"Don't move, Sophie," Bertha said. "You were hurt pretty bad, but you're getting better."

"Where are Heather and Veronica?" Sophie asked.

Bertha turned around. "Gentlemen, would you please go tell Veronica that Sophie is awake?"

"Yes," said Bolt. Sensing that Bertha wanted to be alone with Sophie to explain about Heather, Bolt took Tom's arm and led him out of the room and through Harmony's sitting room.

"What a cold-hearted bitch that Bertha is," Tom grumbled after they left Harmony's living quarters and were walking in the hallway.

"I think you're wrong about her, Tom."

"What do you mean? That woman sat in that room for better than an hour and not once did she show any signs of emotion or feeling for that poor girl. No tears, no sign of concern for Sophie. No damned compassion."

"As it turns out, Tom, I think Bertha has a hell of a lot more compassion than the two of us put together." Bolt smiled at his friend.

"What in the hell are you talking about? Have you lost your mind, too?"

"Maybe, but I've changed my mind about Bertha. She may be demanding, and she may rule with an iron fist, but I don't think she's cold-hearted at all."

"But you saw the way she treated Sophie in there," Tom said, his anger showing on his face. "The way she talked to that poor girl. The way she slapped her around, and pinched her and shook her. That's no way to treat a person as sick as Sophie is. To my way of thinking, that doesn't show any damned compassion on Bertha's part."

"Tom, I think that Bertha knew that treating Sophie roughly was the only way to bring her out of her brutal nightmare. As far as I'm concerned, Bertha is the strong one here."

"Strong?" Tom laughed. "Because she knocked Sophie around?"

"Tom, most women in Bertha's situation would have stood around and blubbered all over everything. But Bertha was strong. She sat quietly for a long time, and then without as much as a whimper, she took charge and did what she knew was best for Sophie."

"Yeah, maybe you're right," Tom mumbled. "The important thing is that Sophie is awake and she's in her right mind."

"That's right, Tom. And from what I saw, I think it hurt Bertha more than it did Sophie."

CHAPTER SEVEN

"Would you two fellows prefer brandy?" Linda asked as the trio entered the parlor.

Tom carried a large silver tray that held five hand-painted demitasse cups, the matching sugar bowl and creamer, silver spoons and small linen napkins. Bolt used two thick pot holders to carry the hot, steaming pot of freshly brewed coffee.

"I'd like brandy," Tom said.

"Sounds good to me," Bolt said.

"Go ahead and sit down," Linda said. "I'll get it." She went around behind the wooden counter of the bar and took a bottle of their best brandy from a shelf, then reached up for the snifters.

Tom carried the tray across the room and set it on the low table between the two sofas. Several small, colorful pillows, most of them made by Harmony, decorated each of the sofas. Bolt placed the hot coffee pot in the middle of the tray, set the pot holders on the table.

"Thanks for the pie, Linda," Tom said as he sank into one of the large, comfortable sofas and stretched his long legs out in front of him. He tucked one of the pillows behind his back, moved the others aside. "Best apple pie I ever ate."

"The whole meal was good, Linda," Bolt said. "Thank you." He settled into the plush sofa opposite Tom.

"You could have a nice supper every night if you weren't so darn stubborn," Linda smiled. She set the bottle of brandy and the two snifters near the silver tray, then poured a small amount of the amber liquid into each of the sparkling glasses, handed one of them to Bolt.

"This is your vacation time, Linda, a time of relaxation," Bolt said as he took the snifter from her. "It's a time for you to do what you want to do, and not concern yourself with our needs."

"But, I enjoy cooking for the two of you," Linda said. "It's not work for me, really. It gives me pleasure to fix a nice meal for you."

"We're big boys now, Linda. We don't need your mothering," Bolt teased. "We're perfectly able to do our own cooking and cleaning."

"You're stubborn, that's what you are."

"You know what, Linda?" Tom sighed.

"What, Tom?"

"Someday, you're gonna make a fine wife for some lucky fellow." He reached up to take the other snifter from her.

She held the glass just out of his reach. "Why, Thomas Penrod, is that a marriage proposal?" she said with a playful smile.

"No, ma'am," Tom said firmly as he sat up and snatched the snifter from her hand. "Just an observation from an idle bystander."

"Oh, Tom, you're a scoundrel." Linda put both hands on her hips and frowned at him. "I don't think either one of you men will ever get married. You're too darned stubborn for your own good."

"Too smart," Tom said.

"Well, I'm not going to give up trying." Linda sat down beside Tom and patted him on top of her head, as if he were a small puppy to be trained.

"Speaking of stubborn," Tom said after he took a sip of the brandy, "that Bertha is as head-strong as they come. She's still insisting that the three of them are going to leave here in the morning. I can't seem to convince her that Sophie's in no condition to travel just yet. Hell, that tomahawk wound'll bust wide open if Sophie rides in the back of that bouncing wagon, and she's too weak to sit up on the driver's bench in front."

"You can't control the old gal," Bolt said. "Bertha says she doesn't want to accept charity from us, so what're you gonna do?" He swirled the brandy around in the snifter, held it under his nose and drank in its sweet, biting aroma before he took a taste of it.

"But doesn't she care anything about Sophie? That poor girl could die if she's moved too soon."

"She cares, Tom. Bertha's just too damned proud to admit that she needs help. I wish she could understand that we're helping her because we want to, because it makes us feel good to do something for somebody who needs our help."

Linda leaned forward and poured herself a cup of coffee, stirred in a spoonful of sugar, then sat back and blew on the steaming cup. "In a way,

Bertha's no different from you two," she said.

"What do you mean by that?" Tom looked over at her, a puzzled look on his face. "No way do I resemble Bertha."

Linda took a sip of the coffee and looked over the brim of the cup at Tom, her eyes twinkling with mischief. "I mean that Bertha won't accept any further help from you because she's too proud, because she doesn't want you to know how helpless she is. And you two won't accept my offer to help you for the same reasons."

"That ain't fair," Tom said. "We're not desperate like those women are."

"Oh?" Linda laughed. "I've heard you grumbling about doing the dishes this past week, Tom. You seem pretty desperate to me."

"It ain't the same, Linda."

Bolt watched the two lovebirds as they became involved in their good-natured bantering, knowing that it was a necessary release of tension for both of them. Tom glanced over at him for some show of support, but Bolt only smiled and sipped the brandy.

"Yes, it is, Tom," Linda continued. "Bertha's denying you the pleasure of helping her when she needs it, same as you two have been depriving me of the pleasure of cooking for you, and washing your dishes and doing your laundry this week."

"You call that pleasure? Washing dishes and doing laundry?"

"Yes I do, Tom. Don't you know that women enjoy doing things for men? We girls derive a great deal of satisfaction from pleasing a man."

"Then you're easily satisfied." Tom drank from the snifter.

"Yes, I am," Linda cooed. "Want to try me?" She nudged her shoulder up against his arm, then pulled away and looked at him coyly.

"Shit, I'll never understand the way you women think."

"You're not supposed to," Bolt said. He took another swallow of brandy, then leaned forward and set the snifter on the table. "Don't try to figure them out, Tom. Just relax and enjoy them. Hell, I learned that much about women a long time ago."

"What did you learn about women long ago?" Veronica asked as she walked into the parlor from the hallway.

Surprised by her voice, Bolt glanced across the room. "Not much, Veronica, that's for sure. How's Sophie doing?" Again, he was stricken with the girl's dark, haunting beauty, and the graceful way she carried herself as she walked toward them. The way the blue robe floated around her, she looked as elegant as any society girl, and yet she had that quality of naivete about her that he liked in a woman.

"She's better, I think." Veronica brushed the loose strands of hair away from her face and sighed with tiredness. "She ate most of the broth Linda fixed for her and now she's asleep. Mama's going to sit with her for a few minutes."

"Would you like some coffee?" Linda offered. "I just fixed a fresh pot."

"Yes, thank you." Veronica glanced at both sofas, as if trying to decide where to sit, then sat down next to Bolt.

"Cream and sugar?" Linda asked as she leaned forward and poured the coffee.

"Just sugar. I'll get it." Veronica spooned the sugar into the cup, stirred it around, before she settled back against the sofa. She tipped her head back for a minute, then raised it. "I didn't realize how tired I was."

As she settled back, a proper distance from him, Bolt smelled a hint of the perfume she had used. "You and your mother had better get some sleep before you fall on your faces," he said with a smile.

"I will. I just want to sit for a minute."

"I'll stay with Sophie tonight and keep a watch over her," Tom offered.

"I don't think that'll be necessary now," Veronica said. "Sophie has passed the crisis."

"I'll sleep out here on the sofa, then," Tom said. "I'll hear her if she wakes up during the night."

"I hope she makes it," Veronica said as she stared into the coffee cup. "She's so weak, so frail."

When Bolt saw Veronica shudder, he glanced up at her face and saw the tears well up in her eyes. He wanted to put his arm around her, pull her close and hold her until her fears went away, until the bad memories disappeared. Instead, he reached over and patted her on the shoulder.

"Sophie's a fighter," he assured the girl. "She'll make it."

91

"I'll say she's a fighter," Tom said. "When Sophie first came out of her deep sleep, she was like a raging bull. For a minute there, I thought she was gonna claw my eyes out, and I think if she'd had any strength at all, she would have broken my nose."

"Yes, Sophie's a fighter," Veronica said with a slight laugh. She wiped the tears away with the back of her hand before they could spill down her cheeks.

"I can't say as I blame her, under the circumstances," Bolt said.

"I can't either," Tom said. "She was out of her head and thought I was that Indian."

"That isn't quite what I meant, Tom," Bolt said with a sly smile.

"Then what in the hell did you mean?"

"Can you imagine what it must have been like for that poor girl to wake up like she did?"

"How's that?" Tom eyed his friend suspiciously.

"Put yourself in her place, Tom. She comes up out of a deep sleep and the first thing she sees when she opens her eyes is your ugly puss. That's enough to scare anyone to death."

Tom picked up a pillow and tossed it. Bolt ducked before it reached its target.

"You two fellows are terrible to each other," Veronica said.

"Tom deserved that, Veronica," Linda said as she picked up another small pillow and clobbered Tom on the top of the head. "Look how ugly he is."

"I never heard you complain before, Linda,"

Tom said as he ducked away from the soft blows. "And here I thought you were sweet on me."

Veronica laughed. "I can see why Linda said you were like a big, happy family here."

"She told you that?" Bolt said.

"Yes."

"And what else did she tell you about life on the ranch?" Bolt glanced over at Linda and she returned his look with a smug, taunting smile.

"A lot," Veronica giggled. "It was girl talk, and quite frankly, none of your business, Mr. Bolt."

Tom laughed. "I guess she nailed your boots to the floor, Bolt. That's what you get for sticking your nose in where it don't belong. Didn't you just tell me not to try to figure women out? Just relax and enjoy them? Try heeding your own advice."

Veronica's mood was cheery and playful and Bolt sensed that they were all feeling the relief from the tension that had mounted through Sophie's crucial hours. And with little sleep during the past few days, Veronica was giddier than the others.

"I reckon she did, Tom," Bolt turned to the tall girl beside him. "I won't pry, Veronica. I'll just assume that since you chose to sit down next to me, it couldn't have been all that bad."

"I'll never tell," Veronica said coyly. She turned sideways and deliberately studied the features of Bolt's face, as if he were a piece of artwork waiting for her approval. "And now that I look at you more closely, Mr. Bolt . . ."

As Bolt watched her appraise him, a smile

93

spread across his face, a grin that was crooked, off-center, as it always was. When he smiled, he noticed that she glanced down at his lips. Her gaze lingered there just long enough for her to trace the line of his mouth and then she raised her head and looked directly into his blue eyes.

An unexpected flush of heat flared up his throat and rose to his cheeks as they gazed into each others' eyes. Suddenly embarrassed, uncomfortable, under her careful scrutiny, he tried to look somewhere else. But he couldn't seem to take his eyes away from her. He felt drawn to her, as if held there by some powerful magnet. The sparks of something magical and mysterious seemed to flow between them as they continued to gaze at each other. It was the hungry, desperate, longing look in her eyes that caused the heat of desire to flood his loins.

He wondered what Veronica was thinking as she gazed into his eyes. Did she feel the same mystical tug that he did, or was she too tired to think? Maybe she was caught up in a trance of exhaustion. She hadn't moved at all since she'd first looked up into his eyes, and although he knew it'd been only a few long seconds, it seemed like several minutes.

No, she wasn't staring at him with a blank expression in her eyes. In fact, she was probably saying more with her eyes than she wanted him to know. It was there, that indescribable magic between them that sometimes happens when a couple looks deeply into each others' eyes and can't hide what they're feeling. He was sure of it, and even more uncomfortable because of it.

"Yes?" he said, finally, and he hoped the husk in his voice didn't show.

"I'll never tell that either," she smiled, snapping out of her fixed stare.

"You were gonna tell me that I'm not as ugly as Tom, weren't you?"

"That, too, is none of your business, Mr. Bolt."

Bolt thought he saw her blush before she turned away to take a drink of coffee from the cup she held in her hand." He straightened up, cleared the husk from his throat as he reached over and poured a little more brandy in his glass. He held the bottle up, nodded to Tom, then added some brandy to Tom's snifter when he presented it.

"Well, now that we've solved all the mysteries of the world, I think you should toddle off to bed now," he told Veronica. "Before you fall asleep sitting up."

She took another drink of coffee, then glanced over at him. "I think I'd like to go outside first and get a taste of the cool night air. It'll make me sleep better."

Bolt wanted to go outside and cool off, too, but he wasn't going to offer to go with her. He didn't trust himself to be alone with her right then.

Bolt had just raised the brandy snifter to his lips when he saw Bertha enter the room. She walked slowly, her shoulders sagging, as if it were an effort for her to take each step. Her eyes were droopy as she glanced over at them.

"Sophie is sleeping peacefully, so I'm going to

95

go upstairs and go to bed," she announced as she walked toward the stairway behind the twin sofas. She reached for the handrail and looked down at the first step, pulled herself up.

"Goodnight, Mrs. Morningstar," Bolt said politely.

"Goodnight," she said. "If there's any change in Sophie, will someone please wake me? I can barely stay awake."

Tom turned around and put his arm on the back of the sofa, looked up at the older woman. "I'm going to be sleeping here on the sofa tonight, Bertha. I'll wake you if the need arises."

"Thank you, young man," she said as she pulled herself up another step.

"Goodnight, Mama," Veronica said. "Sleep well."

Bertha looked down at them. She seemed to notice the brandy snifter in Bolt's hand, and he swore she gave him a dirty look.

"You come to bed, too, Veronica," Bertha said. "Right away."

"I'll be up soon, Mama," Veronica said.

"You come up right now, Veronica," her mother said firmly. "You need to get your sleep so you'll be fit to travel in the morning. It's going to be a hard day for all of us."

"But I had a nap today," Veronica begged. "I'm not sleepy yet."

"That doesn't matter. You come to bed right now, young lady," Bertha demanded.

"Oh, all right, Mama," Veronica pouted. "I'm going to go out and get a breath of fresh air first, so I'll sleep better. Then I'll be right up."

"All right, Veronica," Mrs. Morningstar said as she climbed another step. "Five minutes. No longer."

"Yes, Mama."

"And don't forget to say your prayers before you go to sleep."

"Mama, I'm not a baby anymore," Veronica sighed. "I'm twenty years old now and you don't have to remind me to say my prayers."

"Goodnight, Veronica. You be up here in bed in five minutes." Bertha said as she climbed the rest of the stairs and disappeared down the hall.

CHAPTER EIGHT

"I guess there's no changing Mama," Veronica sighed after her mother was gone.

"I doubt it," Bolt laughed. "She's a strong-headed woman."

"She's just stubborn and set in her old ways," Veronica said defiantly as she set the coffee cup down on the table. "I can't seem to convince her that I'm not sleepy yet."

"She is stubborn," Tom agreed. "I can't convince your mother that she's not going to move Sophie tomorrow morning."

"I know." Veronica shook her head.

"Well, you and your mother can go if you want to," Tom said, "but Sophie's staying right here for at least one more day. Sophie has come through the crisis, but that doesn't mean that she's out of the woods yet. Tomorrow will be her most critical day."

"I agree with you, Tom," Veronica said with an easy smile. "Maybe we can all work on Mama in the morning. It'll take all of us to change her mind."

Linda stood up. "You two think you've got problems. How am I going to convince Tom that he's going to help me with the supper dishes?"

"Oh, no," Tom said. He grabbed a throw pillow and covered his head with it.

"It won't do you any good to hide from me, Tom." Linda laughed as she grabbed the pillow and threw it aside. "You're going with me to the kitchen, Mr. Penrod." She grabbed him by the hands and pulled him to his feet.

"You're vicious, Linda," Tom cried.

"And I enjoy every minute of it," she laughed.

"I'll help you with the dishes, Linda," Veronica offered.

"No thanks, Veronica. You go up and get some sleep. Tom needs the practice." Linda tugged on Tom's ear, playfully dragged him across the room. She turned and flashed a naughty smile just before she and Tom turned down the hall and disappeared from sight.

"You all have so much fun here," Veronica said. "We were never allowed to kid around like that. At least, not in front of Mama. She's always so serious about everything."

"What about your father, Veronica?" Bolt asked. "Was he strict, too?"

"No, Papa enjoyed life more than Mama did, I think. He used to stand there with a smile on his face when he watched us kids romp around in the yard. Sometimes he'd join us in our play. I'm going to miss him, Bolt." She looked up at him and took in a deep breath, let it out slowly.

"I know you are, Veronica. It'll be rough for a while."

"I want to remember the good times," she said, "not the nightmare of those last few minutes of the Indian raid."

"Then that's what you should think of before you go to sleep tonight. The good times."

"Why does Mama have to insist that I go to bed right now? I'd like to stay up and talk."

"I'm sure she's just thinking of your welfare, Veronica," Bolt said gently.

"I'm beginning to wonder if it's my welfare or hers she's more concerned with," the distraught girl said sadly as she shook her head. "Mama wants things her way all the time, and it seems that she's satisfied only when everything is in order around her. For her to be happy, everything has to be done how she wants it, and when she wants it. Otherwise, she's solemn and bossy."

"And you do everything you can to please her, don't you?" Bolt's words were accusatory, and that's the way he meant for them to be. He was trying to get Veronica to see that she was allowing her mother to control her life. Bertha was strong, yes, but Veronica would have to speak up if she wanted her mother to stop treating her like a child.

"Yes, of course." Veronica gave him a puzzled look. "All children are raised to obey their parents, aren't they?"

"Yes," Bolt laughed. "That's because parents have experienced enough of life to know what's best for their children. They don't want their children to get hurt. But just remember, there always comes a time when the mother bird pushes her baby out of the nest to fly on his own."

100

"I know what you're trying to say, Bolt, but Mama will never change. Not in all her born days. That's just the way she is. She's got her own ideas about how things should be done and she doesn't allow anyone else to express their opinions or feelings. What about me? What about the way I feel? Doesn't she care?"

Tears sprang to Veronica's eyes and Bolt knew that she was overly tired.

"Maybe your mother cares too much about you, Veronica."

"Then why won't she allow me to make my own decisions? I'm not a little girl who has to be told what to do." Veronica brushed the tears away.

"Right now, I think you've reached the point where you're so tired and punchy, you can't think for yourself," Bolt said. "We all get that way sometimes, and maybe your mother is wise enough to know that you need sleep."

"Yes, I know I'm tired," Veronica said, "but why can't I decide when to go to bed? I talked to Mama before and I can't seem to convince her that I'm not sleepy yet. She just doesn't understand that if I go to bed now, I'll just lie awake and think about the ... the ... I'll just think about Papa, and Tommy, and Heather and all the rest of them."

"I know this is a difficult time for you, Veronica, but I think if you can get some sleep tonight, you'll feel better in the morning."

"But Mama's always like this, Bolt. It's not just tonight. When is she ever going to realize that I'm a grown woman now and that I'm perfectly able to know what's best for me? It's no use, she'll never change." Veronica's voice was full of despair.

"Then maybe you're the one who has to change, Veronica. Not your mother," Bolt said.

"How can I do that?"

"Maybe you just have to go ahead and make your own decisions and let your mother know that you plan to stick to them."

"Oh, Mama wouldn't like that at all. She'd think I was disrespectful."

"Maybe that's a chance you have to take, Veronica. You might be surprised. She might respect you for standing on your own two feet." Bolt reached over and picked up his snifter, took a small sip.

"That smells good. Could I taste it?" Veronica asked.

"It's pretty strong," Bolt said.

"Just a taste?"

"I don't know. I wouldn't want your mother to think I corrupted you, but go ahead if you want to. Just remember, if you make your own decisions, you're responsible for your own actions."

Veronica leaned toward him and sniffed the glass. Her hand brushed against his when she tilted the glass up and took a small swallow.

Bolt watched her as her eyes went wide. She opened her mouth to speak, but no words came out. She patted her chest and swallowed again.

"Are you all right?" he asked.

"Yes. It took my breath away," she said. "Why didn't you tell me it was so strong?"

"I tried to warn you," he laughed, "but you wouldn't listen." He set the snifter on the table and stood up. "Now you trot yourself upstairs, young lady, and get some badly-needed sleep."

Veronica got up from the sofa and put her hands on her hips, so that her elbows formed small wings. She glared at Bolt. "Now you're telling me to go to bed. You and Linda, and Mama. You all think you know what's best for me. Well, maybe I'll just be as stubborn as Mama is."

"Veronica, please, you need the sleep."

"I'm going outside for some fresh air, Bolt. Would you care to join me?"

"You are a stubborn little wench, aren't you?" Bolt laughed. "Yes, I'll go out with you for a minute." He bowed and gestured her toward the front door.

"Thank you, kind sir," she said as they stepped out into the cool night air. The moccasin slippers Linda had loaned her from Harmony's closet whispered across the wooden planks.

Bolt had lit the kerosene porch lantern on his way into supper and its light now spread across the wooden planks. And on the hill above the bordello, a ray of golden lamplight spilled from one of the windows of the ranch house. He had left the lantern burning, the wick turned down low, when he had been up there to change clothes before supper.

The moon was just beginning to show above the horizon and Bolt knew it would be almost full tonight.

"I'll only stay for a minute," Bolt said as he followed Veronica over to the porch railing.

"And then what?" Veronica turned and smiled at him.

"And then, since I have to get up with the chickens to get the chores done, I'm going to march on up the hill to my ranch house and go to bed. You can stay up all night if it pleases you because there won't be anyone around to tell you what to do. The rest of us will be asleep."

"I just may do that," she laughed. "Is that your house up there?" she asked, nodding toward the lamplit window.

"Yes. That's where I hang my hat."

"How come your house is way up there on the back of your property?"

"That's the front of my property," Bolt said. "Just beyond the house is the road that leads to San Antonio."

"I guess we came in the wrong way."

"Right through the pasture."

Veronica leaned against the railing, tilted her head back and breathed in the night air.

Bolt looked up at the stars that dotted the dark sky and listened to the night noises. Except for the constant hum of the crickets and the croaking of the frogs down by the stream, the night was quiet around them. A cool breeze blew across his face and carried her delicate scent to his nostrils.

"It smells good out here, doesn't it?" she sighed. She turned to look at him and the lamplight danced in her dark eyes and accented the mole on her cheek. Her robe was held in place by a sash and the top of it fell open just enough so that he could see a hint of cleavage in the dim light.

"Yes, it does," Bolt said.

"Have you ever slept out under the stars?" she asked as she looked up at the sky.

"Many times. Tom and I used to be cattle drovers before we bought the ranch and we've spent many a night sleeping out on the trail."

"You and Tom have been friends for a long time, haven't you?"

"For as long as I can remember. We grew up together."

"Is your father really a preacher, Bolt, or did you just make that up to please my mother?"

"My father's a preacher. I don't make up fibs so other people will like me. I am what I am and you can take me or leave me. It's your choice."

"I like that. Do you have any brothers or sisters?"

"A brother. He's married and lives near my father in Kansas."

"Do you ever see them?"

"Not very often. It's been a couple of years."

"I can't imagine what it's going to be like with just Mama and Sophie and me left," Veronica said as she looked up into Bolt's eyes. "Nothing seems real to me any more when I realize that I'll never see the others again."

"I know, Veronica. Things will never be the same for you, and as you go through life, you'll learn that nothing ever stays the same. You've got enough spunk to go on and make a new life for yourself and I know that some day, you'll find happiness again."

"Oh, I didn't want to talk about these things," Veronica said with a shudder.

"Maybe you need to talk about them if they're bothering you."

"But it scares me to think about the future. I just don't know what we're going to do."

The breeze caught a loose strand of Veronica's hair and blew it across her face. Without thinking, Bolt reached over and brushed it back. He was stunned by the warmth and softness of her flesh. Before he could withdraw his hand, Veronica grabbed his wrist and held his hand there.

"Your touch feels good," she said with a sudden urgency to her voice. She pressed his hand against her cheek and purred like a kitten.

"You feel warm," he said as he withdrew his hand. "Have you got a fever?"

"No, it's your hand that's warm," she said with a smile. "That's why it felt so good against my cool cheek."

"Hmmm, I thought it was the other way around."

"No, Bolt. Just standing here next to you, I can feel your warmth."

"I didn't know it showed," he said, smiling selfconsciously.

"Why does everybody call you Bolt?" she asked.

"I guess because that's my name."

"But it's your last name, not your first."

"It sounds better than Jared, doesn't it?"

"Yes, I guess it does," she laughed. "It's more fitting anyway."

"Whatever that's supposed to mean."

"Bolt is a strong name, and I think you're a strong man."

"Well, thank you, ma'am. Has anybody ever called you Ronnie? Short for Veronica?"

Veronica's smile faded away and a dark cloud seemed to come over her face. "Just one person," she said after a minute.

"Your father?"

"No," she said with a heavy sigh. "A very special friend of mine. His name was Raymond Pelkner."

"Was he your beau?"

"I suppose he was, for a short time. Ray worked for my father and for a long time, we were just friends. But our friendship grew and so did our love for each other, and that's when he started calling me Ronnie. Only when we were alone. About three months ago, we decided to get married."

"But you didn't."

"No. I tried to tell Mama about my feelings for Ray, but she just brushed them off, saying I wasn't old enough to know my own mind. She said I wasn't even to think such thoughts because Raymond wasn't good enough for me anyway. But he was. Ray was a good man, a decent man, and a hard worker, like my father."

"Why didn't your mother like him?"

"It wasn't that she didn't like him. In fact, she

treated him like a son. It's just that she wanted me to marry someone who was better off financially than anyone who lived in our village."

"Mothers are like that with their daughters, I guess," Bolt said. "No fellow is ever good enough for them."

"It's funny, in a way," Veronica said with a smile. "My family lived in that little village all my life and I often wondered how I was supposed to meet this wealthy stranger Mama wanted me to marry."

"Maybe she thought he'd ride into your village and sweep you up in his arms and carry you away on his white horse."

"I suppose so. But I wish I had listened to my heart instead of my mother. Ray died in the Indian attack and he's buried along with Papa and Johnny. I'll always regret that I didn't marry him. And I'll always blame Mama for that."

"Is that why you're so bitter about your mother telling you what to do?"

"I didn't know I was bitter."

"It shows, Veronica," Bolt said in a gentle voice. "You flare up like a kicking donkey every time she tells you to do something, even if it's for your own good."

"I guess you're right, Bolt."

"You can't go on blaming your mother for all your disappointments in life. It isn't fair to either one of you. If you start making your own decisions, then you won't have anyone to blame but yourself if things don't work out the way you want them to."

"You make it sound so easy, Bolt, but it's hard to change. I don't know if I can."

"You've already made a start," Bolt smiled. "Now, you'd better go in and get some sleep. It's time for me to head up the hill."

"But I'm not sleepy," she said.

"Well I am. Stay up if you want to, but I'm going to bed. Goodnight." He turned and walked toward the stairs. He heard Veronica's moccasins shuffle across the wooden boards behind him.

"Bolt, would you take me up to see your house?" she asked.

The question caught Bolt off guard. He swung around and looked at her. The lamplight reflected the pleading in her dark eyes. If she only knew how much he wanted to hold her in his arms, he was sure she wouldn't have asked.

"Not tonight, Veronica. Maybe in the morning."

"We might not be here in the morning, Bolt. Why not tonight?"

"Because I'm tired and you're tired, and I don't want you falling asleep up there. I'd never be able to explain that to your mother," he said, trying to make light of the situation.

"Mama has nothing to do with this," she said. "I just want to see your house."

"Why? It's just a house, Veronica."

"It's your house, Bolt."

The way she said it tugged at Bolt's heart. He felt his pulse quicken. "Not tonight, Veronica," he repeated.

"Please, Bolt," she said as she took his hand. "I won't stay long. I promise. I just want to be with you for a little while longer."

He looked into her eyes and knew he couldn't deny her.

"You're stubborn, Veronica."

"Then I can come?"

"Yes," he said. "But just for a little while."

"I promise you won't be sorry," she said as she squeezed his hand.

There was no mistaking the urgency of the husk in her voice.

CHAPTER NINE

They walked up to the big ranch house, hand in hand, so Bolt could guide Veronica along the path that was unfamiliar to her. He was glad that he and Tom had built the wooden steps on the path. The moon was not high enough in the sky yet to shed enough silver glow to light their way and the handrails helped.

At the top of the steps, they made their way to the back porch and climbed a short flight of steps. Once inside, the light from the burning lantern allowed them to go through the entry hall and on into the kitchen.

"Oh, I like your kitchen," Veronica said as she looked around the large room with the cooking utensils hanging from nails on the walls.

"It's nothing fancy," Bolt said. He watched her face glow with enthusiasm as she studied the cook stove and the painted wooden cupboards, the crystal and china that sparkled behind the window of the china cabinet. He smiled when he saw her walk over and run her hand across the lace tablecloth that Harmony had crocheted for him.

111

As he watched her move about the room, he realized that she was still in the nightgown and the blue robe that Linda had found for her to wear. He had become so accustomed to seeing her that way all evening, he'd forgotten about it, and again, he felt slightly uncomfortable. It had been different when the others were around, but now it seemed improper. Especially knowing that if Bertha wasn't asleep, she could come looking for her daughter at any time.

"Oh, I think it's pretty fancy," Veronica said. "The kitchen is huge."

"It's just a farm kitchen."

"I love it. It's so cheery in here with those yellow curtains and the yellow pads on the chairs and all your nice china."

She was obviously impressed by what she saw and he wondered what kind of a home she had lived in.

"I guess women notice those things," Bolt said as he picked up the lantern and carried it to the far end of the room where there was an open door that led into one of the hallways. "You want to go into the living room?"

"I want to see the whole house, Bolt," she smiled. "The living room, the bedrooms. Everything. That's why I came up here."

"The bedrooms, too? Bedrooms are bedrooms. They're all alike."

"Yes," she said. "I've never had the opportunity to walk through a bachelor's house and I'm curious about how you live."

112

"I reckon we live the same as you women do," he laughed. "And, remember, two lazy bachelors live here, so you'll have to forgive the mess."

"I'm not looking for dirt, Bolt. I just want to see how you've got your place decorated."

As they walked down the hall, her delicate scent seemed stronger in the narrow passageway.

"What's in there?" she asked as they passed a closed door.

"Tom's bedroom." He opened the door, held the door open so she could look inside.

"I'll agree. Tom's a little messy," she said with a smile when she saw the unmade bed and the stack of dirty laundry in the corner of the room.

"If you think that's a mess, then I'd better not show you my bedroom. You'll think I'm a pig."

"That's the room I'm most interested in, Bolt," she said with a coy smile.

Bolt had a funny feeling in the pit of his stomach. As before, he didn't know if she was flirting with him or whether she was just genuinely curious and naive in her way of expressing herself.

"That's the living room," he said as they passed the large open room at the front of the house. "You can look at that later."

He held the lantern out in front of him as he turned down another hallway. He figured it was best to show her his room first and end up in the living room, rather than walk through the living room and end up in his bedroom. He didn't want to be put in a position where she would think he

113

was trying to take advantage of her.

"Well, this is my bedroom," he said when he reached his room. "Go on in and have a look." He stood in the doorway and held the lamp out so the light would spill into the room.

"You're not nearly as messy as Tom is," she said as she inspected the room. "You've even made your bed."

"Well, don't look too closely at the floor. I've got things scattered all over the place."

"This room is full of man smells," she said as she sniffed the air.

Bolt laughed. "I don't know if that's good or bad."

"It's good," she said. "I like the way you smell. This room smells like hair tonic and cigar smoke."

"I rarely smoke a cigar, and never in here," he smiled. "I think it's your imagination."

"Maybe so, but I like it."

"Are you through looking around?"

"For now," she said.

Bolt didn't know what she meant, but he was relieved to get away from the bedroom. He quickly escorted her back through the hallway, glad that she hadn't noticed the closed door of the third bedroom, where Harmony sometimes slept, and which was strictly feminine.

When they entered the living room, he set the lamp down on an end table and walked across the room to light another lamp. The flame flickered for a minute and when he turned the wick up, the room was bathed in a radiant glow.

"Oh, I love your living room. It's so big and airy," she said as she made a slow circle around the room, pausing to look at the bookshelves and the rolltop desk, stopping to study the pictures on the wall. She looked at the massive drapes that covered the windows. "It must be lovely to sit in here during the day with those big windows. And it must be cozy in here when you have a fire in the fireplace."

"We like it," Bolt said. He walked over and sat down on the sofa.

"The whole house is decorated to suit a man's taste, isn't it?" she commented as she completed her tour. "The leather chairs and sofa, the plain drapes at the windows instead of frilly curtains, the pictures on the walls."

"I should hope so," Bolt laughed. "What'd you expect?"

"Well, I've never been in a home that didn't have a woman's touch. I know that woman, Harmony, I think her name is . . . I know she cooks and cleans for you two fellows and I thought maybe she had added some of her own touches."

"No. Harmony cooks for us and cleans the house, but she doesn't concern herself with the way Tom and I live up here."

"That's good." Veronica strolled over to the sofa and sat down at the other end. "Linda said that Harmony was someone special."

"She is," Bolt said with an uneasy smile. "Tom and I don't have much time for housework and

Harmony keeps this place running. Especially when Tom and I have to be gone for several weeks on a cattle run."

Veronica folded her hands in her lap and stared down at them, suddenly quiet.

"What's on your mind, Veronica? You want to talk about it?"

She turned to face him. "Yes," she said. "I've been thinking about Heather and I just can't get her out of my mind. With Papa and Johnny, and the others, I know they're dead and buried, but with Heather, I just don't know. I feel guilty because I'm not out there looking for her."

Bolt reached over and placed his hand on Veronica's hands, gave them a reassuring squeeze. "I know this has been hard on you, but don't feel guilty. You did what you had to do by getting your mother and your aunt away from the Indians."

"Bolt? Do you know anything about Comanche Indians?" She placed one of her hands on top of his and stroked it, her mind many miles away.

"A little."

"Do you think there's even a slight chance that my sister is still alive?"

"There's always a chance, Veronica. The very fact that the Comanches took Heather with them instead of raping her and killing her on the spot is a good indication that they wanted to keep her."

"So they can violate her. That's the only reason they want to keep her, isn't it?" Her hands began to tremble as she spoke.

"I know this isn't easy for you to talk about, Veronica, but, yes, the Indians would rape her, I'm sure."

"Oh, I just hate to think about what poor Heather has gone through. At least the others didn't have to suffer very long."

"Sometimes Comanche braves take their trophies back to their village and present them to their chief, to win coup, to show they have good medicine. A white woman would be considered a very special trophy."

"I don't understand any of that," she said as she looked up into his eyes, an apprehensive look on her face.

"If she was presented to the chief of the tribe, then he would be the only one to rape her. That's bad enough, but it could be worse. Would you rather not talk about it, Veronica?"

"No, I want to know," she said as she continued to stroke his hand. "If she wasn't given to the chief, then what would happen to her?"

"Then I'm afraid the other braves would have their way with her."

"All of them?"

"Yes, probably."

"And then what would happen to her?"

Bolt could barely stand to look at the pain in Veronica's eyes. He tried to be as gentle as he could with her.

"They would keep her until they tired of her."

"Would they torture her?"

117

"Not the braves, except for raping her. It's the squaws who torture captured white women."

"How? How do they torture them?"

"I don't think you want to know, Veronica."

"Yes, I do. I've pictured the Indians cutting off her fingers, or her breasts, or scalping her while she's still alive. I've imagined them burning her at the stake or putting her in a pot of boiling water." Veronica's whole body began to tremble.

"Oh, you poor girl. You've put yourself through so much. You shouldn't think about such things." He took his hand away from hers then pulled her close to him and tucked her under his arm.

"It's hard not to think about it, Bolt," she said as she shivered against him. "I've got to know what could happen to her so I can put the nightmares out of my mind. That's why I can't sleep tonight. Please, go ahead and tell me how the squaws torture white women. I don't think it could be any worse than what I've already imagined."

Bolt took a deep breath. "Squaws torture their prisoners by beating them with sticks. By throwing rocks and dirt at them. By spitting on them. They would probably tie a white woman to a long rope so she couldn't get away and they would feed her as if she were a dog, by throwing scraps of food on the ground in front of her. They would probably kick her and hit her if she disobeyed, or if their moods were bad."

"But Heather wouldn't know their language,"

Veronica said with desperation. "She wouldn't be able to understand what they wanted her to do."

"I know. That's why the squaws kick their prisoners, or beat them with sticks. To make them understand. Indian women are really more cruel than the braves."

"Then I hope Heather was given to the chief. That wouldn't be quite so bad, would it?" Veronica asked hopefully as she searched Bolt's eyes for some reassurance.

"Often times, that would be a worse fate, Veronica. If the chief has many wives, and he usually does, they would become very jealous of the white woman who was pleasuring their husband. The chief's squaws can be particularly cruel."

"Oh, I can't bear to think about it," Veronica said as a shudder coursed through her body. "Maybe Heather's better off if she's already dead."

"It's better to think that your sister escaped from the Indians right away and that she's now living some place where she's safe. Like you and Sophie and your mother are."

"I want to go looking for her," Veronica said. "I want to know for sure."

"I can help you," Bolt said.

"Oh, I'd be forever grateful." Veronica snuggled up closer to him.

"Hold me tight, Bolt. I'm so scared for Heather. I need to be held."

Bolt pulled her even closer to him and felt the

quivering of her body. He tucked her head against his chest and wrapped both arms around her.

"Go ahead and cry, Veronica."

"I'm all cried out, Bolt. I don't have any tears left."

He held her in his arms and rocked her back and forth until the trembling finally subsided. He brushed her long hair away from her face, then lowered his head and kissed her on the forehead. She responded by squeezing his arm.

After a few minutes more, he eased his arms away from her and helped her to sit up straight. He cupped his hand under her chin and lifted her head so he could look into her eyes.

"I think I'd better take you back down to your place now, Veronica, so you can go to bed. Maybe you'll be able to sleep now."

"Bolt?" she said with a pleading look in her eyes.

"Yes?"

"Will you make love to me?"

Bolt was stunned by her words. Despite his intentions to be a perfect gentleman in her company, he felt the hot twinges of desire flood through his loins. As if it had a mind of its own, his shaft pulsed and began to thicken.

"Veronica, please, I don't think you realize what you're saying."

"Yes, I do, Bolt," she said as she gazed into his eyes. "I need you. I feel very mortal tonight."

"You need to be held and cuddled, and reassured that life is real. I can understand that, Veronica," he said gently. "And I'll hold you as long as you want me to."

"I want you, Bolt. Please don't turn me down." She tipped her head back and waited for his kiss.

Bolt bent down and kissed her tenderly. Her lips were soft and pliable under his gentle caress, and when he felt the warm dampness of her mouth, his growing manhood burned with desire.

She turned slightly and thrust her breasts against his chest. Soft mewling sounds escaped from her throat as she pressed against him.

Bolt no longer fought his conscience. He wrapped his arms around her and held her tight. And even before he backed away from the kiss, he knew it was already too late for either one of them to change their minds.

"I love the way you kiss," she said in a husked whisper. "You're so tender with me. Your lips are so soft." She raised her head up for another kiss, parted her lips invitingly.

"I hope you know what you're doing," he said with a lust-cracked voice, just before he smothered her with another kiss. He slid his tongue between her lips and plunged deep inside where it was hot and moist. He was surprised when she responded with her own flicking tongue.

"Yes, I do," she panted when they broke for air. "I want you inside of me."

Bolt wanted her so badly he could hardly breathe. He sucked in the air, but before he could answer her, she plied his mouth with another burning, passionate kiss.

He felt her hand slip inside his trousers and his knees went weak. When she found his cock and wrapped her hot hands around it, he thought he'd explode right then. His mind danced with the pleasure of her sensual touch.

"You don't know what you're doing to me," he said as their lips were still touching.

"Yes, I do," she whispered, and then plunged her tongue into his mouth.

Bolt moved his hand around and pushed her robe off one shoulder. He tugged at her thin gown, tried to find a way to get inside, then finally used both hands to unbutton the front.

Veronica moved her head back and glanced down as he cupped a bare breast in his hand. She pushed his head down, urged him to take a nipple in his mouth. He sucked on the soft flesh until it turned to a rubbery nub.

While he suckled, she quickly freed herself of the robe, then slowly tugged the skirt of her gown up until her dark nest was fully exposed.

Bolt slid his hand down across her furry mound and found the dampness between her legs. She jerked at his touch, made little gurgling sounds in her throat like a purring cat. And then her hips started undulating as he slid his finger into her damp slit.

"I want you now, Bolt. Please," she said with a sudden urgency as she withdrew her hand from his trousers.

"I want you, too, Veronica," he said. "I want

122

you very much."

They came together in a wild, passionate kiss that sealed their fate. They were a mass of arms and legs as they tried to get closer to each other.

Veronica was the one to break the kiss.

"Please, Bolt," she cried desperately. "I can't wait any longer to feel you inside me."

"I want you so much," he said as he peppered her face with hot kisses.

"Take me to your bed, Bolt," she begged. "Please take me to your bed."

CHAPTER TEN

The cool breeze chilled their still-damp bodies as they made their way back down the steps to the log cabin an hour later.

Bolt was still weak and out of breath from the extreme pleasure she had given him. She had been like a wild, starved tigress with him, romping over and under his body, squirming beneath him until the sheets were a rumpled mass.

She had consumed him totally, like no other woman had done, sucking every ounce of strength out of him in her effort to please him, milking every pleasure she could for herself. It had been a mutual thing between them and he had put his best effort into it, knowing that she was caught up in her own needs. He was surprised that she could still stay on her feet.

"You were so good," she said as they reached the bottom step of the path between the two houses. "Thank you, Bolt."

"The pleasure was mine, believe me," he said as

124

he took her arm and escorted her across the yard that was now bright with the moonlight.

"You made me feel alive again."

"You're very sweet, Veronica."

"So are you. You're the kind of tender man that every girl dreams of."

"You say things like that and I'll take you back up to my house," he teased.

When they reached the bottom of the steps, Bolt glanced up at the house and saw the light spilling from the parlor windows. As far as he could tell, there were no lamps lit upstairs. At least not in the bedrooms in the front of the house, and he didn't know which rooms Linda had put Veronica and her mother in.

"I hope your mother isn't awake," he whispered. "She'd have my hide if she knew that I'd taken you up to my place."

"I don't really care any more," Veronica said with a smile. "You didn't attack me. I did the asking and I don't regret it in the least. And as far as Linda is concerned, I think she would understand."

Despite her brave talk, and despite the fact that she was wearing moccasins that made little sound on the boards, Veronica tiptoed across the porch.

Bolt turned the doorknob slowly and pushed the door open quickly so it wouldn't squeak. He saw Tom sitting on the sofa, playing a game of solitaire on the low table in front of him. He was relieved to see that Tom was the only one in the parlor.

"How's Sophie?" Bolt asked.

"Sleeping like a baby," Tom said as he pushed the cards aside.

"Is Mama asleep?" Veronica asked.

"Yes. I haven't heard a peep from her since she went to bed. Except for her snoring."

"Then she's sleeping deeply."

"I assume you finished the dishes, Tom," Bolt grinned.

"Yes. And I assume you took care of things up at the house."

"Yep."

"You have a lovely house, Tom," Veronica said. "You'll have to learn to make your bed."

Tom glared at Bolt. "What were you doing in my bedroom?"

"We didn't go in your room, Tom. Veronica wanted to see the house and I showed it to her."

"Well, I didn't know how long you two would be gone. I was just about ready to blow out the lamp and go to sleep."

"You'd better go to bed, Veronica," Bolt suggested. "If we can't convince your mother to stay an extra day, you may be facing a hard day."

"I'm on my way," she said as she headed for the stairway. "But I plan to sleep late in the morning. Mama can leave if she wants to, but I'm staying here with Aunt Sophie."

"Goodnight, Veronica," Bolt said. "I think you made the right decision."

"So do I," she smiled. "Goodnight, boys. Sleep

tight." She waved, then walked on up the stairs and disappeared from sight.

"Tom, I want you to ride into town with me tomorrow afternoon," Bolt said.

"Why? What's going on in town?"

"There's a chance that Veronica's sister, Heather, might still be alive and I want to ride out that way and see if I can find her. I want to go into San Antonio tomorrow to see if we can round up some good men to ride with us."

"Us? You expect me to go chasing after wild Indians?"

"Of course, Tom. I wouldn't want you to miss the fun."

"Shit! That doesn't sound like my kind of fun. Plowing into a herd of savage, murdering Indians."

"It's serious, Tom, or I wouldn't ask. I don't want to get the girls' hopes up, but after talking to Veronica just now, I think there's a pretty good chance Heather is still alive. The Comanches wouldn't have carted her off if they had planned to kill her, would they?"

"No. That ain't their style," Tom said. "From what Bertha told me, it was a small band of Indians who attacked them. Maybe ten or twelve of them. She said they carried nothing more than their weapons, so I don't think they'd want to bother with excess baggage unless they had a use for it back at camp."

"That's what I figured. You'll go with me, won't you?"

"Yeah, I'll go," Tom grumbled. "I ain't lookin' forward to it, but we'll have to try to find her before they've used her up."

"I knew you'd understand."

Tom shook his head. "Damnit, Bolt. I told you the minute those gals rode up, you'd get us in a heap of trouble."

"We're not in any trouble," Bolt said.

"It's gonna be dangerous, ain't it?"

"It could be."

"Danger. Trouble. Same difference as far as I'm concerned."

"Thanks, Tom. I knew I could count on you to ride with me. Goodnight. Sleep tight."

Tom picked up a pillow and threw it at Bolt, just in time to hit the closed door after Bolt had ducked outside.

"Goodnight, Bolt," he muttered to himself as he blew out the lantern and crawled under the covers on the sofa. "Sleep tight. It's for certain I won't."

"But I'm not going, Mama," Veronica told her mother over breakfast.

The two women had slept late that morning and the others had already eaten by the time they came downstairs. Bolt and Tom were out near the stable tending to their chores. Linda had stayed in the house long enough to prepare breakfast for Veronica and her mother, and then she had gone outside to gather the eggs. Sophie was asleep, so the women were virtually alone in the house.

"Yes you are, young lady," Bertha insisted. "We asked these people for food and a place to spend the night. They've been more than kind to us and we can't impose on them any longer."

"They don't care if we stay, Mama. In fact, they want us to stay until Sophie is better."

"That would be taking advantage of a kindly deed, and I won't hear of it," Bertha said.

"We aren't really imposing, Mama. They have plenty of room for us."

"I said we're leaving this morning and that's final."

"But think of Sophie. She's better this morning, but she shouldn't be riding in the wagon just yet. She's still very weak and we don't want to risk having that wound break open. Sophie really needs to stay in bed for another week."

"San Antonio isn't such a long journey from here," Bertha said. "Maybe an hour, or less."

"What am I supposed to wear to town? This borrowed robe and nightgown?"

"Mercy, no," Bertha said. "In fact I was shocked when you came downstairs in that outfit last night. It's not a proper thing for a lady to wear in front of gentlemen. Don't you know that parading around in skimpy clothes like that can give men immoral ideas? Even decent men like Bolt and Tom."

"Oh, Mama, they didn't think anything of it. They understand our situation."

"Still, that's no way for a daughter of mine to dress in polite company. You embarrassed me, Veronica. As soon as you finish breakfast, I want you to go upstairs and put on that frock you were wearing when we got here yesterday. That'll do you until we can get you something else to wear."

Veronica felt her temper flare, but she tried to keep it in check. "But my dress is all dirty and tattered. I can't wear that."

"You can mend it and wash enough of the dirt out of it to get you by for now. We won't leave for town until later this afternoon."

"And what are you going to use for money when we get there?" Veronica said sarcastically. "Are you going to rob a bank, Mama?"

"Don't speak to me like that, young lady."

"And don't call me 'young lady' when you're angry with me," Veronica shot back. "My name is Veronica." She was sorry she'd said it as soon as it was out of her mouth.

"Well I never," Bertha huffed.

"Mama, we don't have any money. Can't you understand that?"

"I don't know why you need to be concerned about it, Veronica, but I've already taken care of that matter."

"How did you do that? Did you borrow some money from Bolt or Tom?"

"I certainly did not. I wouldn't think of such a thing. We're already obligated to them."

"Then what are you going to do?"

130

"Tom told me about an inexpensive boarding house in San Antonio. I'll work it out with the owners so we can earn our keep until we get on our feet."

"Well I'm not going."

"You're being stubborn, Veronica, and I won't have it."

"No more stubborn than you are, Mama. I have to do what I think is best for all of us, same as you do. We can't seem to agree on this matter, so I guess we'll have to go our own ways."

"I won't have you defying me like this."

"Well, I'm not going with you, Mama. You go ahead and go to San Antonio by yourself, if you want to, but Sophie and I are staying here for a while."

"No, you're not. You're both coming with me."

"Mama, I'm not going to let you risk Sophie's life just to save your own pride."

"What's gotten into you, Veronica? You've never talked to me this way before."

"Maybe I should have," she sighed, suddenly tired of arguing with her mother.

"Veronica! What's wrong with you? Has the shock of this ordeal been too much for you?"

"I'm not tetched in the head, if that's what you mean. I know you're a proud woman, Mama, and I have always admired you for that. I just think you're wrong in this case."

"You have no right to decide what's right or wrong. I'm the one responsible for our survival and I'll make all the decisions."

"That's not fair, Mama. I'm a grown woman now and I have just as much right to express my opinion as you do. That's all I'm trying to do, but you won't listen to me. You never do."

"I won't tolerate your insolence any longer, young lady. You'll do what I say."

"There you go again. My name is Veronica. You ought to know. You named me."

"How dare you speak to me that way! I'm your mother, after all."

"Then maybe that's where I got my stubbornness," Veronica said. "I certainly didn't get it from Papa's side of the family."

"Veronica! You hush your mouth!"

Veronica saw the shocked look on her mother's haggard face, the pain in her eyes. She was truly ashamed that she had hurt her mother like that, but she knew she had to put her foot down right then or she'd never be able to crawl out from under her mother's protective wing.

"Mama, I'm sorry if I've hurt you, but I've made my decision and I'm sticking to it. Aunt Sophie and I are staying here for the time being. At least until she's well enough to travel." Veronica stood up and started to clear the dishes from the table.

Bertha remained at the table. She lowered her head and stared down at her lap for several minutes. When she looked up again, Veronica thought she saw tears in her mother's eyes, something she couldn't remember ever seeing before.

"Veronica, maybe I'm the one who is tetched in the head," she said, her voice soft and gentle. "Maybe this ordeal has been too much for me. I just want to push on and on and on. I want to run away from the grief because I don't know how to face it like you do." The tears spilled over the brims of her eyes and trickled down her wrinkled face.

"Oh Mama, don't talk that way," Veronica said as she rushed over to her mother and patted her on the head. "You've been so strong and brave throughout this whole thing."

"No, I haven't been brave or strong, Veronica," Bertha said stubbornly as she rose from the table. She shook her head. "I didn't even try to save my own daughter when the Indians attacked." Bertha's body shuddered as she began to sob. "I was too scared to move. Sophie had to do it for me and now she's suffering because of my cowardice."

"Mama, don't blame yourself for what happened. You were too shocked to move after you saw Papa and Tommy on the ground like that. I was, too. My legs just wouldn't move. Sophie reacted differently to the shock, that's all. You can't carry that guilt around with you."

"But I can't even cry for Papa and Heather, and my sweet little Tommy," Bertha sobbed, the tears flowing freely now. "I don't have any feeling left. No sadness. No grief. No love. I'm just all cold and empty inside."

Veronica wrapped her arms around her mother

133

and pulled her close. "You're crying now, Mama. You're crying for all of them. Papa. Tommy. Heather. All of our dear friends. You've kept the grief buried deep inside you too long. Go ahead and cry."

Wracked with heaving sobs, Bertha threw her arms around Veronica and buried her head in her chest. "Oh, I love you, my pretty daughter," she cried.

"I love you too, Mama." Veronica gave her mother a squeeze and wiped her own tears away.

CHAPTER ELEVEN

"What're you gonna do now?" Tom Penrod asked as he and Bolt headed back to the Rocking Bar Ranch late that evening. It was nearly midnight and with the light of the moon shining across the landscape, they could already see their ranch up ahead.

Sensing that they were almost home, the horses picked up their pace. The two men rode side by side, except that Bolt's horse, Nick, pranced out a shoulder's length ahead of Tom's sleek animal.

"I don't know, Tom. Try again tomorrow, I reckon. I thought for sure we'd find a few hard-cases who'd be eager to ride with us."

Tom spit a big wad of tobacco to the ground and with his horse now at a gallop, the breeze caught a spray of the sticky brown juice and splattered it across Tom's face.

"Damnit," he muttered.

"What's the matter?" Bolt asked. He turned his head and glanced back over his shoulder at his long-time friend.

"Just a little tobacco juice," Tom said as he wiped his sleeve across his speckled nose and cheek.

Bolt laughed. "You're supposed to chew that stuff, Tom, not use it as shaving lather."

"Go to hell, Bolt." Tom brushed at the small, damp stains on his shirt.

"I'm sure glad I wasn't riding downwind." Bolt faced forward again and glanced at the ribbon of road ahead of them.

"You know something, Bolt," Tom said after a minute. "Now that we know that it's a brutal band of renegade Comanches who are attacking the small villages, I'm not sure I want to go either."

Bolt shook his head. "You didn't expect them to be a band of friendly Indians, did you? After what they did to Veronica's family?"

"I was kinda hoping they'd be on the friendly side," Tom said meekly.

"Well, if we can't find anyone to ride with us, we'll just have to go out there and face those damned Comanches ourselves."

"All twelve of them? I don't like the odds."

"We got no choice, Tom. We've got to find Heather." Bolt turned his horse off the main road and onto the path that threaded through his yard, past his ranch house, and on down the hill to the stable and barn.

"But it'll be like looking for a needle in a haystack," Tom grumbled. "Those damned Comanches could be anywhere out there. We're talking about a lot of country to cover."

"Tom, we talked to several fellows tonight, in three separate saloons, in fact, who had heard about that particular group of Indian renegades who attacked the Morningstar village. You know how news travels when you're riding the trail. A couple of those men said they had actually witnessed the aftermath of one of the Comanches' brutal attacks. They had smelled the smoke from the burned-down buildings. They had seen the bloody bodies lyin' on the ground. They had smelled the stench of death."

"Yeah, they seemed to know what they were talking about. At least they all told basically the same story about those fuckin' renegades."

"That's right, Tom. They all agreed that the renegade band worked both sides of the border around Eagle Pass. Veronica and her family were from a village near Uvalde. Those Comanches shouldn't be too hard to track down."

Bolt eased up on the reins and let Nick have his head as the horse trotted down the hill. He glanced across the yard and was glad to see that there was no light spilling from the windows of the bordello. Everyone would be asleep that time of night.

"If they're so damned easy to find, then why hasn't someone put their lights out a long time ago?" Tom said, bouncing in the saddle as his horse followed Nick down the hill. "From what I heard tonight, those fuckin' bastards have been working the same territory for nearly a year now."

"I don't know, Tom," Bolt said as he climbed down from his worn leather saddle and patted his horse on the rump. "You heard the reaction we had from those fellows tonight. Even though they're a rough bunch of hombres, they're all scared to death of those Comanches renegades."

"And yet you expect the two of us to go out there and face 'em alone. No, sir. Not this little doggie. I ain't goin' out there chasin' after that bunch of crazy redskins."

"We'll just have to catch 'em when they're off guard. Maybe we can find their village and sneak up on 'em when they're not armed."

"You really think those savage renegades live in a village?" Tom asked. "I'd think they'd be roaming the land all the time, lookin' for new towns to torch, fresh scalps to dangle from their trophy lines."

"They'd have their own village to go home to, Tom. It's the nature of violent killers like that to have a place where they can go and live like normal people after the brutality of their raids. I'm sure we can find them."

Tom reined his horse to a halt next to Bolt's animal. He climbed out of the saddle and walked around to face his friend. "I think you're daydreaming if you figure the two of us can take on a dozen murdering bastards and still come out with a full head of hair. You know what happened to the people of Veronica's village and there were more than three dozen people there."

Bolt stepped inside the dark stable where the odor of manure and hay was strong. One of the horses already bedded down in the stable for the night snorted from its stall. Bolt lit the lantern that hung from a peg near the doorway, then led Nick to his stall. "Those poor people were caught off guard when the Indians attacked their village," he said as he uncinched the saddle thongs. "We'll be prepared."

"I don't think there's any way to prepare for meetin' up with those bastards. And I still don't like the odds."

Bolt carried the saddle to the back of the long, hay-strewn room and set it on a barrel. "Well, we can't just forget about Heather, can we, Tom? As long as there's a chance she's still alive, we've got to try to find her."

"It's useless, Bolt. We both know she's already dead." Tom spoke as he dragged his saddle down from his animal's back and put it away. "According to Sophie, those Comanches travel with nothing but their ponies and their weapons. They're not gonna want to tote around excess baggage."

"I still think they took Heather back to their village. Otherwise, why would they have carried her off the way they did?"

"Because they saw Sophie and realized they hadn't killed everyone in the village," Tom said as he added water to the bucket in his horse's stall. "I figure they hauled her off a short distance away from the smoldering village, took turns climbing between her legs, then slit her throat and left her for buzzard bait."

"Could be."

"Hell, for all we know, those renegades could have traded Heather to some outlaws for a couple of jugs of rotten tanglefoot."

"Maybe." As they finished tending to their animals, Bolt strolled over to the lantern and turned the wick down. The flame flickered for an instant, then went out.

"Hell, she could be anywhere out there, Bolt. But my gut feeling is that she's already dead."

"Then maybe we can find her body," Bolt said as they walked out into the moonlit yard. "At least that way we'd know for sure, and it would put everyone's mind at ease."

"It's just plain stupid to go out there, Bolt," Tom argued. "Tell me, what are our chances of finding a body in that vast wilderness?"

Bolt stopped and looked at Tom. "Not very good," he admitted.

"Besides that, I doubt that the Comanches would take the time to bury her ravaged body, even if they had a notion to. If her body was lyin' around out there, the wild animals would have feasted on it by now. It's useless, Bolt. Give it up."

"I won't give it up until I've done everything I can to find her, Tom. If someone had stopped those damned renegades when they torched their first village and scalped their first inno-

140

cent victim, Veronica's family would be alive today."

"Then let the government send in some U.S. marshals to track 'em down," Tom said. "That's what they're getting paid for."

"Tom, you've got more damned excuses than a frigid wife."

Tom gave Bolt a sideways glance. "Maybe that's because I don't want anyone messing with my private parts. Especially renegade Indians."

"Well, if you can come up with a better idea, Tom, let me know." Bolt turned and started to walk away.

"The bordello is dark and quiet tonight," Tom commented as he looked across the large expanse of tall grass that glimmered with a silver sheen in the moonlight. "Everyone must be asleep already."

"Which is exactly what I plan to be within the next five minutes," Bolt said as he continued walking toward the steps that would take him up the hill to the ranch house.

Tom chuckled to himself. "All hell's gonna break loose tomorrow, isn't it?" he said as he traipsed after Bolt.

Bolt stopped in his tracks. He turned around and found Tom right behind him. "What is it, Tom?" he sighed.

"Well, the other five harlots are coming back from their vacations tomorrow and they're gonna be all rested and primed to get back to

141

work tomorrow night."

"I hope so," Bolt snapped. "Maybe we can all get back to some sort of a normal routine around here."

"It could prove interesting when that homey log cabin over there suddenly turns into a smoky, raucous brothel. I can see it now," Tom laughed. "Fellows swarming into the parlor, the gals struttin' around in their sexy little outfits, and Bertha Morningstar and her daughter right smack-dab in the middle of the action."

Bolt had been thinking about the same thing and figured that was probably why he was so irritable tonight.

The Morningstars had been here a little more than twenty-four hours and already they had disrupted his life so that he and Tom were not getting the chores done. And with Harmony planning to be gone yet another week, he was discovering that he and Tom couldn't even keep up with both the housework and the ranch chores. Trying to solve the Morningstars' problems only added to their burden.

For instance, instead of making their beds and cleaning up the kitchen after lunch and doing the stacks of laundry as they'd planned, Tom and he had ridden into town to try to round up some men to help them find Heather. And here he was now, planning to ride halfway across the country, plunge into the midst of a band of infamous savage Indians and valiantly rescue a young girl he didn't even know. Maybe Tom was

142

right. Maybe they should just let it go. It wasn't his problem, after all, and he couldn't devote his whole life to rescuing every damned damsel in distress.

And he got a sick feeling in his gut when he realized that he might be stuck with Bertha and the girls indefinitely.

"I'm sure the sparks will fly tomorrow night, Tom," he said, with no enthusiasm. "Now if I could just get to bed, that would help."

"What are you gonna do, Bolt? Keep the bordello closed until the Morningstar women leave? With Sophie so sick, it might be a few days."

"No, Tom. We open tomorrow night, as scheduled. It'll be business as usual. If our guests don't like it, they can leave."

"You can't let 'em leave here with no money and no food, no place to go."

"Why not?" Bolt said. "That's the way they came to us, and Bertha's too damned proud to accept our help. For all I know, they may have already left."

"You think so?" Tom glanced toward the dark bordello.

"Maybe. You know Bertha was insisting on leaving today and I don't really think Veronica's got the guts to stand up to her mother. She's been made to kowtow to her mother all her life and I don't think she can change overnight, although I think she wants to."

"But as sick as Sophie is, I don't think Linda would have let Bertha take Sophie away."

143

"I don't know, Tom. We haven't seen them all day. They were still asleep when we went over there for breakfast this morning and we didn't stop back by before we rode to town."

"You want me to go over and see if they're still here?"

"Makes no difference to me. I'm going to bed."

"You didn't tell them about the bordello, did you?" Tom asked.

"Nope. I figured it was none of their business. If they're still here tomorrow night, let 'em find out for themselves."

"Oh, that ought to be fun." Tom let out a loud whistle. "As religious as Bertha is, can you imagine what's going to happen when she finds out she's been sleeping in a house of prostitution? She's gonna hit the ceiling."

"Maybe it'll knock some sense into that stubborn noggin of hers."

"You sound bitter, Bolt."

"I am. Bertha Morningstar thinks she has to be in control of everybody around her. She thinks that she's right about everything and that everyone else is too dumb to make their own decisions. Bertha is stubborn and arrogant." Bolt stabbed the heel of his boot into the ground and then looked over at Tom. "Just look at the way she's ruined her own daughter," he ranted on. "She's turned Veronica into a helpless, spineless creature who will always tremble as she walks in her mother's shadow. And I'll bet Bertha secretly gloats over the fact that she can

144

make other people feel small and inadequate. Of course she does. It makes her seem more powerful, the ungrateful old bat."

"Jeez, sorry I mentioned it," Tom said as he stepped back.

"Sorry, Tom. I didn't mean to dump all this shit on you. I just get angry every time I think about the way Bertha treats Veronica. In my opinion, Bertha is a very sick woman. I think one of these days, she's going to crack apart, and because of the way she's turned Veronica into a whimpering child, I don't think there'll be anyone around who is strong enough to pick up the pieces and put them back together. Can't you see it, Tom?"

Tom shrugged his shoulders. "I dunno. I just think of Bertha as a stubborn old woman."

"Well, damnit, Tom, Bertha can go ahead and rule other people's lives, but she's not going to rule mine," Bolt snarled. "This is our house, our ranch, and I'm not going to let her control me!"

"The way I see it, Bolt, she's controlling you right now," Tom said in a quiet voice.

"Whatdya mean?" Bolt snapped.

"You've let Bertha Morningstar control your mood. You've allowed her to make you angrier than I've seen you in a long, long time." Tom smiled. "Funny, isn't it? To think how much power a woman like that has over a fellow like you."

"She doesn't have any power over me, Tom. This is my place and I'll do as I please, which

145

includes getting mad if I want to."

"Well, I think you've got Bertha all wrong. I think she's just trying to put on a brave front and do what she thinks is right in order to survive."

"Aw, shit, Tom. What do I know about women? Young or old, I'll never figure them out."

"As you told me," Tom said with a smile, "just relax and enjoy them."

"Goodnight, Tom."

"Goodnight, Bolt. I think I'll go on over to the bordello and sleep on the couch again."

"You want to see if Sophie's still here, don't you?" Bolt grinned.

"I'm a little curious."

"I thought so. Well, don't stay up too late, Tom. You and I are going to put a big kettle of water on to boil in the morning and we're going to wash our clothes. I'm running out of shirts to wear."

"Thanks for spoiling my evening. I'll sure as hell be glad when Harmony gets back."

"Won't we all?" Bolt sighed. "Somebody's got to play hostess when we open the bordello to-morrow night. I think you and I are going to have to draw broom straws to see who wins the honors."

"Let Bertha be the madam," Tom grinned. "Wouldn't that be a sight."

Bolt laughed. "Not a bad idea, Tom. And goodnight for the last time."

The men parted company and Bolt headed on up to the ranch house.

He didn't notice the soft glow in the kitchen window until he was halfway up the steps. He stopped and thought about it as his brow wrinkled to a puzzled frown. He knew he hadn't left a lantern burning. Maybe Linda had come up and lit the lamp for him.

Or maybe someone was in his house.

CHAPTER TWELVE

Bolt hesitated only a minute before he went on up the steps, then climbed the stairs to his back porch. He decided that Linda had come up and left the kitchen lantern burning for him as she had done before.

He noticed that there was something different about the kitchen when he first walked into the large room. As he glanced around, he was surprised to see that it was all cleaned up. All the dishes that he and Tom had left from their noontime meal had been washed and put away. All the clutter in the room had been cleared away, the floor had been swept, the counters scrubbed clean, and the cook stove was spotless.

When he walked across the room, he was even more surprised to see the neat stacks of clean clothes on the kitchen table. They were his clothes and Tom's clothes all mixed up, but clean and neatly folded.

He picked up a folded shirt, brought it up to his nose and sniffed it. He smelled the scent of soap and fresh air, and besides that, there was a hint of perfume in the room.

He stood there for a minute and wondered who had washed the clothes. He didn't think Linda had. She had enough to take care of over at the other house. It had to be Bertha or Veronica. And then he remembered the promise Bertha had made when she had accepted his offer to put the three women up for a night. Of course, it had to be Bertha. She had said that she would do any work she could to pay him back for food and shelter for her and the other two women.

Bolt shook his head as he stared at the stacks of clothes. He smiled and his anger faded away.

"Stubborn old bat," he said aloud.

"Who's a stubborn old bat?"

Bolt nearly jumped out of his skin. He whirled around and saw Veronica standing in the doorway of the hall. She wore only a thin, pink nightgown. No panties, he knew, because he could see the dark thatch of her mound beneath the sheer fabric.

"Jeeez, you scared me, Veronica."

"I didn't mean to," she said as she walked on into the kitchen.

"You should be asleep."

"I'm not sleepy. Besides, I wanted to wait up for you," she said coyly.

Bolt saw the invitation in her sparkling, dark eyes and knew why she was there. "Did you wash all these clothes for us?"

149

"Mama and I did. We cleaned your whole house and both you and Tom have fresh linens on your beds."

"Well, thank you very much, Veronica. I appreciate it, but you shouldn't have done it."

Bolt saw the disappointment in her eyes.

"Oh, I'm sorry, Bolt. I guess Mama and I shouldn't have been up here in your house without your permission. I was kind of hesitant about it, but Mama said you wouldn't care, just as long as we did a good job."

"Oh, I don't care if you and your mother were here," Bolt smiled. "I meant that you and your mother didn't need to do all this work to pay me back for putting you up. I invited you women to stay here at the ranch because I wanted to, not because I felt that I had to."

"And we cleaned your house and washed your clothes because we wanted to, not because we felt obligated," she said with a saucy tilt to her head. She smiled and walked over to the table. "I didn't know which clothes were yours and which were Tom's, or I would have put them away for you."

"I'm not sure myself," Bolt laughed. "We'll sort them out in the morning. God, Tom's gonna be happy about these clothes."

"And you?"

"Of course I'm pleased." Bolt leaned over and kissed Veronica on the forehead. "Tom and I can handle the dirty dishes, and I thank you for washing those, but we're all thumbs when it comes to washing the clothes and hanging them out to dry."

"It's a woman's place to do the cleaning and cooking. You ought to find yourself a pretty young girl and get married, Bolt."

"I should hope that if and when I get married, it'll be for reasons other than just to have someone around to pick up after me."

"How come you've never been married, Bolt?" Veronica blew a strand of hair away from her face and looked into Bolt's eyes.

"I don't think any woman would put up with me, Veronica. You've seen how messy I am."

"Bolt, whose clothes are those in the other bedroom?"

"Tom's," he said, although he knew what she meant.

"Does Tom wear long dresses?"

Veronica looked so concerned, Bolt almost laughed. "Oh, you mean that bedroom. Those are Harmony's dresses."

"I thought Harmony lived with the other girls." Veronica tipped her head to the side and looked at him with a puzzled look.

"She does. Most of the time."

"Then how come she hangs her dresses up here?"

"You're just full of questions, aren't you?" Bolt smiled.

"You don't have to answer, Bolt. I was just

151

curious. I didn't see that bedroom last night and I was surprised to see women's clothing in there when I went in to clean the room."

"Harmony sleeps in there sometimes, when Tom and I are gone for a while. How's Sophie?"

"She's much better today. We had her up and walking around for a while and besides the broth, she ate a little food this evening."

"I'm glad to hear that," Bolt said as he walked over to the counter and poured a glass of water. He drank part of it, then set the glass down. "I thought maybe you'd all be gone when we got back."

"No, but we really do have to leave soon," Veronica said, a sadness in her eyes. "We realize that we have to make a new life for ourselves and Mama thinks she has things figured out so that we can earn enough money to survive."

"I'll bet she has." Bolt didn't mean to be sarcastic, but it came out anyway.

"That's why I came over tonight," Veronica said as she slinked over and kissed Bolt on the neck. "We'll be leaving any day now and I thought this might be the last night I could spend with you. Besides, Linda said the other girls who work here will be coming back tomorrow and I figured it might get too hectic for us to be together."

"It'll get busy once the girls are back, that's for sure. How'd you get your mother to change her mind about leaving today?"

Bolt took another drink of water, swallowed hard, but still felt the flow of heat rush over him. He knew it was from being so close to Veronica. The flowery fragrance of her perfume floated all around him and he found it hard to keep from staring at her beautiful body beneath the thin fabric of her nightgown.

"I did what you told me to do," she said proudly. "I decided that Aunt Sophie wasn't well enough to travel, so I told Mama I wouldn't leave today. She tried her best to get me to go, but I stuck to my decision, like you told me to."

"And it worked?"

"Yes," Veronica nodded. "When Mama realized I wouldn't budge, she agreed that it was best to stay put for a few more days."

"It was easier than you thought it would be, wasn't it, Veronica?"

Veronica gasped as if she were about to cry and Bolt saw the pained expression in her eyes. She turned and as she walked away from him, the flowing gown bounced gently against her firm buttocks.

"No, Bolt. It was the hardest thing I ever did in my life," she cried out as she whirled around to face him. She put her hands to her cheeks and stared down at the hardwood planks of the floor.

"I know it was hard, Veronica," Bolt said as he walked over to her and extended his arms.

"No, you don't know how hard it was," she

said as she stepped back away from him. "Mama's the sweetest person in the world and I said such terrible things to her. I hurt her very badly, I know. Oh, how I wish I had never said those mean, cruel things about her. I just didn't understand her."

Bolt reached over and took both of her hands in his, brought them up and rubbed them against his cheek.

"Maybe they were things that had to be said, Veronica," he said tenderly. "For the sake of both of you. Maybe you said the things that your mother needed to hear."

"But I hurt her, Bolt. It was as though I plunged a knife into her heart."

"Maybe you had to do that, Veronica, to open her heart up."

"But I'm so ashamed of myself."

"Don't be, Veronica." He reached up and stroked her forehead, then tilted her chin up so she was looking at him. "Do you know how we finally brought your Aunt Sophie out of her deep sleep?"

A puzzled look came over her face. "You mean after she went through that spell of being out of her head? Aunt Sophie just woke up, didn't she?"

"Not on her own. Your mother did it, and she did it in much the same manner as you used with her. Bertha slapped Sophie around. She talked harshly to Sophie and treated her more

154

roughly than a sick person should have been. I was shocked at first and I thought your mother had lost her mind. But as I watched her, I could see how much it hurt her to treat Sophie so badly. Your mother shocked Sophie out of her spell."

"I didn't know that," Veronica said.

"And that's all you did with your harsh words, Veronica. You shocked your mother out of her spell."

Veronica took a deep breath. "I'm glad you told me, Bolt. It makes it a little easier."

"How did your mother react when you stood firm with your decision?"

"She broke down and cried. I've never seen Mama cry before."

"She cried because you defied her?"

"No, because she had all that grief and guilt inside her. She felt guilty about Sophie being hurt. She blamed herself for Heather being captured by the Indians because she couldn't save her. She cried for Papa and Johnny and all the rest."

"She needed to cry, Veronica."

"I know that now."

"How's your mother holding up?"

"Mama's fine now, thanks to you."

"You did it, Veronica, not me."

"Mama and I are close now. We were so happy working together today, we actually enjoyed cleaning your house and washing your clothes.

And she wants more than anything for us to find Heather. She has faith now that Heather is still alive."

"I'm happy for you, Veronica." He brushed her hair out of her eyes.

"You're still going to look for Heather, aren't you?"

"Well, Tom and I didn't have much luck today in finding someone to ride with us, but we'll try again tomorrow."

"I want to go with you when you look for Heather, Bolt."

"You can't, Veronica. It'll be too dangerous."

"Well, if you think Mama's a stubborn old bat, you just wait till you're ready to ride out. You won't be able to stop me."

"How'd you know I meant your mother when I said that?"

"Because that's what she was, stubborn."

"And now you're going to be the stubborn one of the family."

"That's right, Bolt."

Veronica threw her arms around Bolt's neck and drew her body up against him. She brushed her lips against his, so delicately, it was like the touch of a butterfly's wing. She thrust her crotch against his growing bulge.

"You're bold," he mumbled as she kissed him again.

"Bold and stubborn. When I make up my mind to do something, I'm going to do it from now on."

"What do you have in mind?" he husked.

"Follow me to your bedroom and you won't have to ask." She grabbed his hand and tugged him toward the hallway.

"You shameless hussy."

CHAPTER THIRTEEN

"Well, it looks like the fun's begun," Bolt commented as he and Tom strolled toward the bordello at dusk. He counted five horses lined up at the hitchrail, switching their tails at pesky flies.

Bolt had been at the bordello for all the hoopla and merriment when the five vacationing harlots returned to the bordello earlier that afternoon. A hired carriage had delivered all five girls to the front door of the big log cabin sometime after noon.

After Linda introduced the excited harlots to the three Morningstar guests, the girls had swarmed over Bolt, showering him with affectionate kisses and hugs. As soon as it was polite to do so, Bolt had made a hasty retreat to the stable so he and Tom could ride into San Antonio.

He left the sleeping arrangements to Linda and she told Bolt that she would have Chet and Rusty bring in a couple of cots from the bunkhouse. She said she would move Veronica into Bertha's room and that Doreen could bunk in with her for a few days.

When Bolt and Tom were in San Antonio, they spent a couple of hours at the stockyards, looking for young drovers who might be eager to earn an extra buck. They had no luck in their search for men to ride to the Uvalde valley with them, so after eating an early supper in town, they headed home. Not more than five minutes ago, they climbed down from their saddles and put their horses in the stable.

"I wonder if any of the girls explained the bordello to the Morningstar women," Bolt said as he and Tom walked across the yard.

"I don't know," Tom said. "Isn't that Veronica and her mother on the porch?"

Bolt peered at the two women who stood at the porch railing. "It sure as hell is."

"You ask me, they don't look any too happy."

"Good evening, ladies," Bolt said when he reached the bottom of the stairs. He tipped his hat, smiled politely. "Nice night out."

Neither of the women responded. They waited until both men were on the porch beside them. Veronica stood with her hands on her hips, her eyes flashing with anger. Her long, dark hair had been pulled back away from her face and hung in soft curls at the back of her head, held in place by a big red bow. Bolt noticed her pretty red dress, buttoned clear to her slender neck, the long skirt full and flared. He realized

159

it was the first time he'd seen Veronica in anything but a robe or a nightgown since she first arrived.

"What's going on here?" Veronica demanded.

"I don't know," Bolt said with a crooked grin. "Tom and I just got back from town."

"I'm going inside, Bolt," Tom said. He tipped his hat to the women, then took quick steps to the door, closing it behind him when he was in the house.

"You know what I mean, Bolt," Veronica said as she leveled her eyes on his. "Those girls in there are all gussied up in their fancy party dresses and some of the guests have already arrived."

"Yes, I saw their horses," Bolt said as he turned and looked at the hitchrail. He heard the soft plodding of hoofbeats and turned the other way to see two more men riding toward the bordello.

"We've been shunned, Bolt," Veronica said, her hands still on her hips. "Mama and I have been treated as if we were lowly house servants."

"What do you mean, Veronica?"

"Linda and a couple of the other girls told Mama and me that it would be better if we didn't attend the party. They said we should stay in our room all evening," Veronica said with a pout. She dropped her hands from her waist and clasped them in front of her. "Linda also said that you would explain when you got back."

160

"Hmmmmph," Bertha snorted. She had a sour look on her face. "I'm not sure I want to attend the party anyway. Those girls are dressed shamelessly. And they've painted themselves up to look like . . . like soiled doves, if you'll pardon the expression."

Bolt removed his hat and held it with both hands in front of him. "That's because they are soiled doves, Bertha. This is a bordello. A brothel. That's why the girls suggested that you stay in your room. They didn't want you to be embarrassed."

Bertha's mouth fell open as she clapped her hand to her forehead. Bolt thought she was going to faint away right there where she stood.

"You mean we've been living in a house of sin?" she exclaimed.

"It depends on how you look at it, Bertha," Bolt said. "I wouldn't call it a house of sin."

"Oh, God, have mercy on our souls," Bertha cried. "Come, Veronica. Let's go to our room where we won't have to be witness to such wickedness."

"Go ahead, Mama," Veronica said as she glared at Bolt. "I'll be along, just as soon as I give Mr. Bolt a piece of my mind."

With her hand still on her forehead, Bertha shuffled to the door. As she went inside, she lowered her hand to cover her eyes.

Veronica watched her mother go, then whirled on Bolt. "Why did you lie to me, Bolt? Why did you lead me to believe that this house was a

161

nice, proper boarding house?" she demanded.

"I didn't tell you it was a boarding house, Veronica. And I didn't lie to you. I answered every damned one of your questions truthfully."

"Then maybe I didn't ask the right questions," she snapped.

"Maybe you didn't, Veronica, but everything I told you was the gospel truth."

"No, it wasn't," she barked. "You told me, in your very own words, that all of the girls who lived here were nice, decent, respectable ladies."

"Those girls are decent, Veronica, every last one of them," Bolt said calmly. "You won't find a nicer bunch of girls in the whole wide west, and I have a great deal of respect for them."

"Decent? Ha!" Veronica said haughtily.

"Yes, decent, Veronica. Some of those girls go to church on Sunday. They cook, and clean, and sew. They gather the eggs and tend to the garden. In the evening, they entertain gentlemen, much like any single girl receives a suitor in her parlor." Bolt spoke casually, trying to explain the situation. "The only difference is that the girls who live here always retire with the gentlemen behind the closed doors of one of the private cottages out back."

"How can you say they're decent when they do such sinful things?"

"You didn't think it was sinful last night, or the night before, when you and I did the very same thing," Bolt said with a smile.

"That's different," she lashed out, her cheeks

162

suddenly flushed the color of her gown. "I didn't do it for pay. You and Tom are nothing but vile men who prey on helpless women."

"I'd say it was the other way around."

"Oh, you're . . . you're hateful," she stammered. "You betrayed me, Bolt. I know now that you've had your way with every one of those wicked women in there and you still took me to your bed."

"I've never slept with any of the harlots who live here," he said.

"I don't believe you!"

"That's your problem."

"After sleeping with such filthy, sinful women, how could you have taken an innocent woman like myself to your bed?"

"You were the one who did the asking, Veronica."

"Oh, you . . . you. . . ." Veronica shook her fists in the air, then clasped her hands together and took a deep breath. "Goodbye, Mr. Bolt. Thank you for your hospitality. I won't see you again. Mama and Sophie and I will be gone at the first crack of dawn in the morning."

"Goodbye, Veronica. It was a pleasure to know you." He smiled and extended his hand.

She glared at his hand, whirled away and stomped toward the door, her nose stuck up in the air.

"Veronica?" he said.

With her hand on the doorknob, she turned only her head. "What?" she snapped.

163

"Go ahead and go to the party if you want to, but don't be surprised if one of the fellows asks you to go to bed with him. You're a very pretty lady. And the way I see it, you're the sexiest woman here."

Veronica's eyes were full of hatred as she turned her head away and dashed into the bordello. She slammed the door behind her.

Bolt worked in the bordello all evening. He stayed behind the bar and served drinks, except for those brief times when Tom stepped in to relieve him for a few minutes.

Being a Friday night, they drew a loud, boisterous crowd, mostly young cowhands who enjoyed a few belts of whiskey after a hard day's work. Bolt stayed busy and so did the girls. As the evening progressed, the room filled with smoke and the stench of spilled drinks. Whenever Tom came to relieve him, he was always grateful for the opportunity to step out on the porch and get away from the deafening noise of the loud laughter and shouting, the almost constant clinking of the piano and off-key singing as the men waited for their turns with the harlots.

It was well after two o'clock in the morning when the last customer left and they finally closed their doors for the night.

Not once did Veronica or Bertha show their faces.

When he climbed in bed that night, he smelled Veronica's delicate scent, which lingered in tthe covers and on his pillow.

He woke up at dawn the following morning and when he and Tom went down to the stable an hour later, he knew that the Morningstar women were still there. Their covered wagon sat just beyond the barn like a sad, neglected hulk.

He avoided the bordello and was glad when he and Tom finally mounted up and rode out to the pasture to check the cattle. They were gone until after two in the afternoon and when they rode back in, he saw that he covered wagon was still there.

"Looks like the women didn't leave, after all," Tom said as they dismounted near the stable.

"It makes no difference to me," Bolt said.

The two men talked about the cattle as they removed the saddles, put the horses in their stalls and gave the animals fresh food and water. When they were through, they stepped outside.

"I wonder if Sophie took a turn for the worse," Tom said as he glanced across the yard at the large, two-story log cabin.

"Go on over and see, if it'll put your mind at ease," Bolt said. "I'm going to stay down here and work."

"What're you going to do?" Tom asked as he looked at Bolt.

"Just straighten up the stable, fix a few things that need fixin'."

"Well, if you don't need my help, I think I'll mosey on over there."

"Go ahead," Bolt laughed. "You won't be happy until you do." He watched Tom walk across the field, then turned and strolled back into the stable, picked up a broom.

For the next fifteen minutes, Bolt was lost in his own thoughts as he puttered about the stable. He was just about to pound a nail in a loose shelf when he sensed someone's presence in the room. A brief shift of light? A certain smell? A sound? He didn't know what made him feel that way, but he knew someone had entered the stable quietly.

His hammer still poised in his hand, he turned around and saw Veronica standing at the far end of the room, just inside the wide, open doorway.

"I thought we already said our goodbyes," he said abruptly. He glanced at her for only an instant before he turned his back to her and drove the nail home.

"You really work here, don't you?" she asked. "Both you and Tom."

"Of course we do," Bolt said without turning around. He picked up another nail, set it in place. "There's a lot of work to raising cattle." He slammed the hammer down on the head of the nail, hit it square, tapped it in with three more short blows.

"Do you always wear a pistol?" she asked. She walked over to a nearby feed barrel and sat down, fluffed her skirt out around her.

"Most of the time." Bolt moved to the other end of the shelf, set another nail in place.

"Why?"

"Rattlesnakes. Coyotes." He still didn't turn around.

"Bolt, what was it like down there last night?" Veronica swung her dangling legs back and forth.

"Down where?" he said after he hammered in another nail.

"In the ... the parlor?"

"Noisy."

"I know that. I could hear the noise until the middle of the morning. I meant what was it like. A Greek orgy?"

"I don't know, Veronica. I've never been to a Greek orgy."

"Well, what did everybody do?"

Finished with his chore of securing the loose board, Bolt set the hammer down and turned around. "If you were curious about it, you should have come downstairs and seen for yourself."

"Oh, I couldn't do that. What do girls feel like when they make love to a stranger?"

"I don't know. I ain't a girl." Bolt glanced around the stable, didn't see what he was looking for. He walked on past Veronica, went outside and rummaged through a pile of various-sized leather thongs.

Veronica slid off the barrel and followed him

outside. She watched him sort through the leather strips. "Do the girls enjoy doing it? Do they get any pleasure out of it?" she asked as she looked over his shoulder.

"I don't know. I never asked." Bolt pulled a thong out of the pile, held it up, measured it by eye, tossed it back down.

"Are the girls ever scared?" she asked, hovering over him.

"I don't know." Bolt dug out another leather thong, shorter and wider then the first one, and decided it would do.

"But some men are cruel, aren't they?" Veronica said. She studied the thong Bolt held up, as if she were involved in the selection process. "Don't they hit the girls sometimes? Or slap them around?"

Bolt stared directly at Veronica for the first time. "Not in my bordello, they don't."

"But I've heard that some men are always brutal with their women," Veronica continued. "Aren't your girls worried that they'll be tortured by some man with a sick mind?"

Bolt's eyes narrowed. "If any customer hurts as much as an eyelash on one of my girls, he's kicked out on his ass." Bolt carried the thong into the stable. He walked back to a large wooden plank that served as his work area and set the strip of leather down.

Veronica trotted after him. "You serve liquor here. What about the men who are nice enough when they come in and then turn nasty after a couple of drinks?" she asked. "Isn't there a chance they could hurt one of your girls?"

"If a customer gets drunk, he's escorted out the front door and told not to come back until he can behave like a gentleman." Bolt placed the thong on top of a wooden box that was missing its handle, decided the strip was too short, after all. He went back out to the pile of loose thongs.

Again Veronica followed him outside. "Why do those girls do what they do?"

"I don't know." Bolt felt the pangs of irritation begin to claw at his stomach muscles.

"Why do you have a brothel out here?" Veronica asked. "Why do you allow such things to happen in one of your own homes?"

Finally fed up with her continuous questions, Bolt stopped what he was doing, stood up straight and turned to face her.

"It's a long story, Veronica, and as you can see, I'm busy," he said coldly. "As for the gals, you'll have to ask them why they do it. But remember, it's personal and none of your business."

Veronica tipped her head back and took on an air of haughtiness. "I would never have given myself to you if I had known you slept with whores."

"I don't know the difference between a whore and any other woman," he said, "but I told you I don't sleep with any of the harlots who live here."

"But you must!" she exclaimed.

"No, I mustn't," he said. "I slept with you because you wanted me to, and because I wanted to. Now, if you're expecting any pay, you should have mentioned that beforehand."

"Oh, you!" Veronica turned and stalked off. After several steps, she turned around. "You can forget about going after my sister. I'll find Heather myself!"

"Fine with me, lady. Goodbye and good luck!"

CHAPTER FOURTEEN

Bolt didn't walk down to the bordello until well after nine o'clock that night. It was Saturday night and since they expected an even bigger crowd than the night before, Tom had offered to watch over the girls and serve the drinks during the earlier hours of the evening.

He heard the din òf the noisy crowd as soon as he stepped out onto the back porch of the ranch house. And as he walked down the steep steps of the path, he saw that both hitchrails were lined with the horses that belonged to the customers. Thirty horses, he figured, and the night was still young.

The loud, droning cacophony swelled around him as Bolt entered the open door of the bordello. He blinked his eyes in the smoke-filled parlor and glanced around the room as he threaded his way to the bar.

In the blur of the browns and blacks and whites that the men wore, he caught a glimpse of something red. As he sorted out the red object, he was startled to see Veronica Morningstar sitting in a straight-back chair in the far corner of the room. Three men hovered around Veronica, obviously enjoying themselves.

"Damn her. What's Veronica doing here?" he asked Tom as he walked around behind the crowded bar.

"She's waiting for you, Bolt," Tom said as he passed a tumbler of whiskey over the counter to a waiting customer.

"Why? So she can flaunt herself in front of me? So she can get her revenge because I ignored her this afternoon?"

"I don't know her reasons, Bolt. She just said she wanted to talk to you. Do you want me to wait here while you go see what she wants?"

"To hell with her."

Bolt glanced over at her and saw that she had already spotted him. He watched as she pushed through the men, pausing to smile sweetly at those she bumped into.

"Bolt! Bolt!" she called from behind the men gathered at the bar. She waved her hand in the air.

Bolt ignored her call.

She pushed on through until she stood facing him.

"Bolt, I need to talk to you," she said.

"I don't think we have anything to talk about."

"Please, Bolt. It's important."

"Go ahead," Tom urged. "I'll stay here."

Reluctantly, Bolt went around the bar and escorted Veronica out on the porch where they could hear each other.

"What'd you do, decide to find out for yourself what it was like to be a whore?" Bolt said sarcastically.

"Why, Bolt, I do think you're jealous."

"What's so all-fired important you've got to talk to me tonight? We're busy in there."

"I wanted to ask you if you'd still be willing to go looking for Heather."

"You told me to forget it, and I have."

"Please, Bolt," Veronica begged. "I know Heather's still alive. I need your help."

"Yeah, I guess so. I was sort of planning to go anyway," Bolt said.

"Then, you'll really do it, Bolt? You'll go looking for Heather?" Veronica cried, her eyes full of anticipation.

"Yes. I thought Tom and I would head out early in the morning. I'm not promising anything, but we'll find her if we can."

"I'm going with you, Bolt."

Bolt frowned at her. "You can't, Veronica. It'll be too dangerous."

"I don't care how dangerous it is," Veronica said firmly. "It's my sister and I'm willing to risk my life to save her."

"I know how you feel, Veronica, but you stay here. It's a hard trail out there. Tom and I are going to have to move fast and you'd just slow us down."

"No, I wouldn't, Bolt. I'll bet I can outride either one of you. And I know that country out there. I can be a big help."

"We may get into a situation where we have to fight for our lives. We can't be worrying about you."

"I can shoot straight," Veronica said. "I can take care of myself."

"I didn't know you were so talented."

"I'm going with you, Bolt. I've made my decision and I'm sticking to it."

"You're stubborn."

"Yes, I am," Veronica smiled.

"You can go on one condition."

"What's that?"

"You have to promise that you won't ask any more of your silly questions," Bolt said. "I just couldn't take it."

"I promise."

"Can you be ready to go shortly after sunup?" Bolt asked. "It'll take us a little time to pack after the sun comes up in the morning, but I want to get an early start."

"I'll be ready whenever you are." Veronica's face beamed with excitement. "I'll have to wear this dress Linda helped me make yesterday. It's the only thing I've got to wear besides that tattered old frock I was wearing when we got here."

Bolt glanced down at the new dress. "Don't wear that red dress, for godsakes. We want to sneak up on those renegades, not flag 'em down. Just wear you old dress. I'll take along an extra pair of my trousers and a shirt for you to change into along the trail."

"Do I need anything else?"

"No. I'll bring an extra coat for you. It might turn cold on us," Bolt said as he ran things through his mind. "No perfume. We want to smell like the land itself. And wear comfortable shoes. I think that's all. Tom and I will pack the guns and ammunition and the rest of the supplies."

"What about food?" she asked.

"I've already got that packed. The first couple of nights we'll be able to build a fire and cook a hot meal, but as we get closer we'll have to forego the fire and eat cold food. Jerky and hardtack, mostly."

"I didn't realize there was so much you'd have to do before we started out," Veronica laughed. "I just thought we'd get on our horses and ride toward the west."

"We've got to be prepared for any contingency. That's how we get the edge on the renegades. Are you sure you don't want to stay behind and let Tom and me take care of it?"

"No, I want to go. Thank you for helping me, Bolt. You're a good man." Veronica leaned forward and kissed Bolt on the cheek.

"I hope we can find Heather," Bolt said. "Now you'd better go up to bed and get some sleep. Dawn comes pretty early."

"Bolt, could I play the piano for your guests before I go to bed?"

"You play the piano, too?"

"Yes. Mama always played the piano for our church services. She taught me."

"Why do you want to play the piano?"

"I don't know. I guess I just want to be a part of things."

"That's a strange thing for you to say, Veronica. You were so opposed to the idea that this was a bordello and that the girls who lived here were harlots. Now you want to be a part of it." Bolt shook his head. "I'll never understand you women."

"Well, I don't want to do what your girls do," she said with a shy smile, "but I feel like I want to participate in some ways. I waited for you in the parlor for two hours. I sat in that chair way back in the corner so the men wouldn't think I was one of the working girls."

Bolt tilted his head and gave her a questioning look. "Oh? When I walked in, it looked like there were three fellows who were bidding for your affections."

"Oh, Bolt," Veronica laughed. "They were waiting for the other girls. They were just talking to me to pass the time, and they were all gentlemen. Until they came up, shortly before you got there, I was all alone. I had a lot of time to sit there and observe the things that went on in the parlor. It was different from what I had expected."

"In what way?"

"Well, I thought the men would be rude and vulgar. I thought they'd be dirty and foul-mouthed."

"We get those kinds, especially after they get a couple of drinks in their bellies."

"I'm sure you do, but I expected every man

who visited a bordello to be a dirty old lecher. The men who are here tonight seem to be clean and neatly dressed. Oh, I heard some naughty talk, but for the most part, the men were polite and cheerful. I was surprised to hear the men standing around in small groups talking about politics or business."

"Most of the men who patronize whorehouses do it because it's the only place they can go to satisfy their needs. If it weren't for places like this, there would be a lot more rapes, a lot more violence toward women."

"I'm beginning to understand that now," Veronica said. "Why didn't you explain all this to me this afternoon when I asked."

"Maybe you had to see it for yourself."

"I guess I did. Even though I knew what the girls were going to do when they led their customers toward the cottages out back, it didn't seem to offend me as I thought it would. I guess that's because I got to know the girls this afternoon and they're all decent, just like you said they were."

"I'm glad you feel that way, Veronica."

"It seems like a big party in there, and I just wanted to be a part of it for a little while. That's why I wanted to play the piano."

Bolt put his hand on Veronica's shoulder and led her toward the door. "You can play for a few minutes only, Veronica. And then you go to bed."

"I will. I promise, Bolt."

Inside, Veronica settled on the piano stool and

straightened her skirt around her legs as Bolt took up his post behind the bar. She sat up straight, poised her fingers over the keyboard, then began to play.

The tune was instantly familiar to Bolt and without putting a name to it, he started humming along as he wiped the counter with a towel.

Others recognized it too. Heads turned in her direction. Men stopped talking and wandered over toward the piano. Some started to sing the words and within a brief space of time, most of the customers had gathered near the piano to sing the words, "Onward Christian Soldiers."

When she finished the song, there was a long uproar of clapping and happy laughter, a feeling of merriment in the room. Veronica glanced around and smiled. She played the song again and this time, everyone in the room clustered around the piano and either sang or hummed along with the music.

By the time Veronica finished the song for the second time, Bertha Morningstar was standing in the middle of the stairway, clutching her dark, thick, woolen robe about her neck.

"I knew it!" the older woman exclaimed. "I knew that was you playing that piano, Veronica. What are you doing down there?"

"Just entertaining the gentlemen, Mama," Veronica called out. With all the men clustered around her, she couldn't see her mother and she knew her mother couldn't see her.

Bolt cringed. He knew what must be going

through Bertha's mind. He dashed toward the piano as the others stared up at Bertha and began to move away.

"You get up here right now and go to bed," Bertha demanded in a loud voice. "No daughter of mine is going to entertain men in a brothel."

"Aw, Mama, we're just having fun," Veronica shouted. "The men are enjoying it and so am I. Can't I play a little longer?"

Laughter rippled across the room.

"No!" Bertha said. "You get up here right this minute."

Bolt took Veronica by the arm, urged her up off the piano stool. "This time I think your mother's right," he said as he headed her toward the stairs.

Halfway up, Veronica paused on the steps, turned around and waved at the friendly men. They responded with a round of applause.

Bertha reached down and grabbed Veronica's hand and pulled her up the stairs. The applause didn't stop until the two women were out of sight.

"Why'd you send her upstairs?" Tom asked when Bolt got back to the bar.

"Because she needs her sleep. Same as you do, Tom," Bolt answered. "You'd better go up to the house and get some sleep."

"It's Saturday night, and you ain't my mama," Tom said.

"Then don't blame me if you're tired when you have to get up at five o'clock in the morning," Bolt said. "I've given you fair warning."

"Why in the hell do I have to get up at five o'clock on a Sunday morning, Bolt? It ain't even light out that time of a morning."

"We've got a long ride ahead of us, Tom. I want to get all packed so we can leave as soon as it turns light."

"No. We're not going . . ."

"Yes, we are, Tom. We're going to head out to look for Veronica's sister tomorrow morning."

"Oh, shit! Just the two of us?"

"Actually, there'll be three of us," Bolt said. "Veronica is going with us."

"Oh, that's just dandy," Tom said sarcastically. "You're getting us into a heap of trouble. I just hope you've figured out a way to get us out."

"I hope so too, Tom."

CHAPTER FIFTEEN

"Oh, my God!" Veronica screamed when she saw the bloody battle scene on the flat stretch of land ahead of them. She reined back on her horse, brought him to a halt. "Oh, my God," she said again as she brought her hand up and covered her mouth.

"I count twelve of them," Bolt said as he slid down from his saddle. "There are twelve dead bodies."

"From here, it looks like all of them were scalped," Tom said as he dismounted and walked around to stand with Bolt.

Beyond the bodies stood the pile of charred rubble that used to be a farm house.

It was late afternoon and the weary trio had been on the trail for four long, hard days. Veronica had changed into Bolt's extra set of clothing the first night and found the pants and shirt more comfortable for riding.

This was the first sign they had seen of the

renegade Comanches they were looking for. If indeed it was the same band of treacherous Indians.

"Oh, it looks just like our place did after the attack," Veronica cried. "The bloody, bloody bodies all over the ground, the house burned to the ground. Oh, it brings it all back to me."

Bolt walked over and stood by her horse. He patted her thigh, reached for her hand and squeezed it. "Don't think about it, Veronica," he said.

"I can't help it, Bolt," she said as she began to sob. She took her hand away from Bolt, covered her eyes. "Do you think this was done by the same Indians who killed my family?"

"Probably. How close are we to your village?"

"We're close," she said as she sniffed and wiped her eyes. "Our farm was about ten miles from here, I think."

"Then that means those renegades are working the same territory," Bolt said. "You stay here, Veronica. I want to look around."

Bolt and Tom walked over to the bloody murder scene and milled around the bodies, looking for clues, looking for anything that would help them in their search for the band of renegade Comanches.

"God, how grotesque," Tom said as he stared down at the limp twisted bodies. "Some of them are just children."

"I know," Bolt said. "How can anyone be so sick as to do this? What do they want from it?

It doesn't make any sense to me."

"I don't know," Tom sighed. He turned away, unable to look at the gaping, scalpless faces. "There are hoof tracks all over the place."

"Shoeless hoofprints," Bolt said. "They're Indian ponies."

"The way the prints are scuffed up, there's no telling how many horses there were."

"We're counting on twelve. I hope there aren't any more." Bolt leaned over and tugged at an arrow that jutted from the back of one of the victims. It wouldn't budge so he left it be. "Black feathers with red tips," he said as he flicked the feathers on the end of the arrow.

"It looks like that's the only clue we're going to get," Tom said. "This didn't happen too long ago, did it?"

"Sometime today, I'd say. With all the wild animals we've seen around here, I don't think the bodies would have lasted through the night without having been all chewed up."

"I think you're right, Bolt." He walked away from the mass of human carnage and scanned the ground for more clues, kicking at rocks.

Bolt walked over to the charred remains of the house. He held his hand over the biggest pile, then felt one of the blackened logs. "No heat left. This must have happened before noon."

"Then they're not too damned far away, are they?" Tom said.

"No. They've been gone from here about six hours, I'd guess." Bolt walked away from that spot, stared at the ground as he walked, trying to find a place where the hoofprints separated into individual prints.

"That doesn't help us find their village," Tom said as he continued to scan the ground. "It could be an hour's ride from here, or it could be more than a week's ride."

"Since Veronica's village was not too far from here, I have a hunch that the Comanches have set up camp someplace in the general area."

"You think they set up temporary camps and move them around when they want to strike another area?" Tom asked.

"Could be." Bolt finally found a place where the hoofprints began to separate into individual prints. He stooped down and studied them closer, then followed them out a way. One particular print caught his eye. All of the other prints seemed to go straight ahead and this one looked like it was turned inward, as if the horse were walking on a deformed ankle. He walked a little further and found another print that looked the same. "I think I have something here, Tom."

"What is it?" Tom turned and came over to Bolt.

"Look at that print. It looks like one of the horses might have a bad ankle."

"Yeah, I see it," Tom said. He continued to walk slowly, peering at the ground. "Here's another one."

"Well, that's not much to go on," Bolt said as he stood up and flexed his shoulder muscles. "If

184

the hoofprints hold up, we could follow them straight to their village."

"Bolt, come look at this," Tom said. "What do you make of it?"

"What, Tom?" Bolt said as he walked over and looked at the ground. "That's one of their feathers. Black, with a red tip. Stuck straight in the ground, in the middle of a bunch of small pebbles, as if it were put there on purpose. They marked this spot." He leaned over and started to pick it up.

"Wait, Bolt. Look at the way those pebbles are arranged. Doesn't it look like the shape of a deer, or an elk?"

"Hmmmm. It does," Bolt said. "A deer, or an antelope. It sure as hell is a rock drawing of some four-legged animal. And look where they've stuck the feather."

"Right square in the heart of the animal," Tom said.

"Looks like they've left their calling card."

"Let me see it," Veronica said as she rode up. "Listening to you two talk, I just remembered something."

The boys stepped back. "Does it look familiar?" Bolt asked.

Veronica's eyes lit up. "Yes. I remember seeing it now," she said. "I didn't see it as an animal's shape at the time, but when I went out searching for survivors after the attack, I remember seeing a little stack of pebbles on the road in front of our house. I thought at the time that some of the children had put them there."

"Was there a feather like this one?" Tom asked.

"As a matter of fact, there was," Veronica said. "It was on the ground near the pebbles. It wasn't sticking up like that one is."

"It looks like we're on the right track," Bolt said. He leaned over, snatched the feather, and stuck it in his pocket. "Let's go."

"We won't build a fire tonight," Bolt said as they dismounted in a stand of cottonwoods that was way off the beaten track. "I think we're getting close."

It was already dark out and the diminishing moon provided them with the only light they would have that night.

They had followed the Indian pony hoofprints for only fifteen minutes before the tracks fanned out in several different directions. Bolt knew that they had split up to confuse anyone who might be tracking them. For a while, they followed the hoofprints of the pony with the deformed ankle, but finally lost the tracks when they led into a stream. Although they spent another hour riding up and down the stream's edges, they never did pick up the trail again.

They each removed their bedrolls from behind their saddles and spread them out on the ground, with Veronica's blankets in the middle, as they had been doing every night on the trail.

Bolt dug into his saddlebags and brought out the two wads of rolled cloth that contained the beef jerky and the hardtack. He offered them to Veronica, who was sitting on her blankets. "Not much of a supper," he said, "but it'll get us by."

"Thanks. This is fine," she said as she took one of each. She passed them to Tom, who sat next to her on his own bedroll. "Do you really think we're getting close to the Comanche camp?"

"Yes," Bolt said as he retrieved the bundles of food from Tom and sat down on his own blanket. "Just a feeling I've got. Something about the smell in the air, or the contour of the land. The land is getting more rugged and the trees are getting thicker. It just feels like the kind of place where the renegades would set up a temporary camp if they wanted to hide out."

"I hope you're right," Veronica said. "I'm getting a little nervous about it."

"I think we all are," Bolt said. "How do you like wearing my clothes?" he asked, deliberately changing the subject. He knew that the sight of the burned-out village had affected Veronica more than she had admitted.

She reached down and tugged at the loose shirt. "Oh, I really like them," she said. "They're a lot more comfortable for riding a horse than that old dress of mine."

"And you don't have to battle that long skirt all day long," Tom said. "I don't see how you women can do anything with all that material around you."

"We manage," Veronica laughed. "But I've got to admit, men's clothes make more sense when it comes to doing chores or riding a horse. Mama would just die if she saw me now."

Bolt's thoughts were already somewhere else. "Tom," he said, "do you remember the name of the chief of this renegade band? One of the fellows we talked to told us and I can't bring it to mind."

"Yeah, let me think a minute. It was something like Deer Run. No. Deer ... antelope. Antelope something. Antelope is in the name," Tom said, thinking aloud. "Running Antelope. Sitting Antelope."

"You're close," Bolt said. "Standing Antelope. That's it, isn't it? Standing Antelope."

"Yeah, that's it," Tom agreed. "I remember now. Standing Antelope. Why?"

"I was just trying to figure out what that pebble drawing represented. And I think that's it. Standing Antelope. Makes sense, doesn't it."

"Yeah, I suppose," Tom said. "But why would the feather be plunged straight into the heart like that? Wouldn't that signify that Standing Antelope was the one being killed?"

"Not necessarily Tom." Bolt drew the feather out of his pocket and turned it slowly in his hand, barely able to see anything but the bright red tip of it in the darkness. "I think it was left there as an invitation, as a challenge, for anyone who considers himself brave enough to try to kill Standing Antelope."

"I think you may be right, Bolt."

"I think these brutal massacres are nothing more than a game to Standing Antelope. I think it's a game of catch-me-if-you-can to him. He sneaks out and slaughters innocent people, torches their homes, leaves his personal calling card in the form of the rock drawings, and then he runs and hides and waits to see if anyone can find him. Hide and seek."

"Oh, that's morbid, Bolt," Veronica said. A shudder coursed down her body.

"Yes, but I think it's true. Are you cold?"

"No, just kind of scared, I guess. Seeing all those mutilated bodies just brought back the nightmare memories of my own experience."

"Why don't you sleep with me tonight?" Bolt said as he put his arm around her.

"Would you mind?" she asked timidly. "I would really feel better if you were close."

"I know. Come on." Bolt lifted his top blanket, crawled inside. He drew her over to him, then dragged her blankets and spread them on out on top of them.

"I feel better already," Veronica said as she snuggled in against Bolt.

"So do I," Bolt laughed. "You'd better get some sleep, too, Tom. I think we're going to have a busy day tomorrow."

"Goodnight, Bolt. Goodnight, Veronica," Tom grumbled as he snatched up his blankets and started to walk away.

"Hey. Where're you going, Tom?" Bolt called after him.

"As far away from here as I can walk," Tom said with a grumpy voice. "Far enough so that I don't have to listen to you two lovebirds all night long. I want to get some sleep."

"A good idea, Tom," Bolt laughed. "We wouldn't want to keep you awake."

CHAPTER SIXTEEN

As Bolt stood on a high ridge and relieved his bladder, he stared down at the thick trees that lined the slope below him. It had been an hour of hard riding since he and his companions had rolled up their bedrolls and ridden away from their camp at daybreak.

He buttoned his trousers and was just about to turn around and walk and back to his horse when he thought he saw a puff of smoke through the shimmering tree leaves. He stopped, bent down and peered through the foliage. He saw it again, a spiral of smoke rising from the valley below.

His heart skipped a beat and then pounded wildly in his chest so that he had trouble breathing. He felt his muscles tense as he walked over to the edge of the ridge and squinted, trying to see what was below him. The trees blocked his view of the valley, but he was sure he'd found what they were looking for.

The Comanche renegade hideout.

He walked a few feet further along the ridge until he came to a clearing. When he stared down into the valley, the sight he saw took his breath away.

There it was, all neatly laid out in front of him. Almost as he had pictured it in his mind when he had thought about the kind of a hideout the brutal, cold-hearted chief would have. A beautiful green meadow, not yet lit by the rising sun, that sat down in the bottom of a deep basin, with steep, tree-lined slopes all around it.

Eleven tepees formed a wide circle in the meadow. In the center of the ring of tepees sat a bigger tepee, black and red designs painted on its animal hide sides, scalplocks dangling from both sides of the door flap.

Although all of the tepees were decorated with similar red and black paintings, and all bore strings of scalps, there was no question in Bolt's mind as to which tepee belonged to Chief Standing Antelope. And if Heather was still alive, he figured she'd be in the big tepee in the center of the ring.

Smoke curled up from the firepit, which was also within the wide ring of tepees. Four thick-waisted squaws tended to the steaming kettles over the firepit. Three braves milled about the center of the camp, near the women, and as Bolt watched, two others emerged from their separate tepees and strolled over to talk to the others. Bolt was too far away to hear their voices. He saw no children at all. At the far end of the meadow, beyond the tepees, more than twenty Indian ponies were confined by a large oval corral.

Bolt tiptoed back through the woods, even though he knew he was too far away to be heard by anyone in the lush meadow valley. He picked his way back to the horses where Tom and Veronica were waiting for him.

"I found the renegades," he said in a hushed whisper.

"Where?" Tom asked.

"Is Heather there?" Veronica asked at almost the same instant.

"Keep your voices low," Bolt cautioned. He looked over at Veronica and saw the apprehensive fear in her eyes. "I don't know, Veronica. I didn't see her. Not yet, anyway."

"Where are they?" Tom asked again.

"They're camped in a big valley, on the other side of the ridge. Mount up and I'll show you." He grabbed Nick's reins, stuck his boot in the stirrup and swung up into the saddle.

"Is there room for us to ride up there on the ridge?" Tom asked.

"Yes, the ledge is wide, probably a hundred feet wide. I think it goes all the way around the valley, like the flat lip of a bowl. I don't know, though. There were too many trees in the way for me to see the whole thing. Hurry. Check your weapons."

Bolt glanced down at his twin Colts, one on each hip. He patted the knife he carried in the scabbard tucked in his waistband.

As soon as the others were settled in their saddles, Bolt led the way and found the same spot on the wide ledge where he had stood only minutes ago. There was a small clearing there, but they eased their animals into the shadow of the trees. From that vantage point, they still had a good view of the entire meadow.

Veronica leaned forward in the saddle and peered into the bowl of the valley. "They're so tiny down there, I can hardly see them," she said, squinting her eyes.

"I know," Bolt said. "It's so far down, the sun hasn't reached the meadow yet. The squaws are fat and the braves are thin."

"I could tell that, but I don't see Heather," she said, her voice tinged with fear. "Do you think she's down there?"

"I hope so," Bolt said. "If she is, we'll do everything we can to get her out."

"I only count seven braves down there, Bolt," Tom said as he rubbed his chin. "I thought there were supposed to be twelve of them."

"The others are probably still asleep. I saw two of them come out of their tepees while I was watching them."

"They sleep late," Tom said.

"Yeah. It looks like they're standing around waiting for breakfast."

"Aren't we going down there to see about Heather?" Veronica asked.

"Not yet," Bolt said.

"I want to go down right now and get her," Veronica said.

"No, Veronica. That would be suicide. We have to wait. We have to watch them long enough to learn their routine."

"We also have to find out how to get down there," Tom said. He glanced around the slopes, looking for a path that led down to the valley.

"Can't we just ride down this slope in front of us?" Veronica asked. "The trees would make good cover for us."

"We could," Bolt said. "It would be slow going picking our way through the trees, and what would we do after we got Heather? If we came back up the same way, those renegades would overtake us before we got half way up. We have to find the path they use."

"They'd have more than one path, Bolt," Tom said as he continued to scan the slopes. "Probably three or four. They're smart enough to leave themselves an escape route."

"Yeah, you're right, Tom."

"Let's go find it, then," Veronica said. "If I didn't think that Heather might be there, I'd ride down there right now and kill every one of those murdering renegades. They killed my Papa and Johnny."

Bolt stretched over and patted the nearly hysterical girl on the arm. "Calm down, Veronica. I know this is hard on you, but we can't just rush into this. We've got to plan it very carefully. Otherwise, none of us will live to rescue Heather."

"I know," Veronica said with a big sigh. "I can hardly stand it, being this close to finding

Heather and still not knowing if she's dead or alive."

"It's tough, Veronica, but please have patience. Heather's life is depending on it, and so is yours."

"Over there, Bolt!" Tom said urgently. His arm shot straight out in front of him. "Straight across the ridge. "It's a scout!"

Bolt craned his neck forward and scanned the rows of trees on the ridge directly across the valley from them. He finally spotted movement, and then saw the Indian on horseback. The brave was as far away from them as the Indians down in the valley, and appeared just as small.

"Yep, that's a scout," he said. "He doesn't seem to be in any hurry."

"There's another one! Off to your left!" Tom whispered loudly. Again his arm shot out and he pointed with his extended finger.

Bolt saw the second scout almost right away. The brave rode in a clockwise direction, as did the other scout. Although he was closer to Bolt and his friends, he was riding slowly away from them.

"I wonder if there are any more," Bolt said in a low voice as he studied the ledge to his right. "Yeah, there's one. High on your right!" This time, Bolt was the one to point.

"Did you notice they're all riding in the same direction?" Tom said. "They must ride in a continuous circle around the ledge."

"I noticed that," Bolt said as he glanced around at each of the scouts. "At the slow pace they're going, it must take them a full hour to make a complete lap."

"That's about what I figure," Tom said as he checked each man. "If those scouts continue riding in that same pattern, that third one over there on our right will be the first one to reach this spot. He's the one we've got to keep our eyes on."

"How long do you figure it'll take him to get here? Twenty minutes?" Bolt asked as he watched the rider.

"About that, which means we'd better start looking for those trails that'll take us down to the meadow. If we ride to the left and stay at their pace, they won't catch up to us anyway." Tom nodded to his left and gave a slight snap to his reins.

"Yeah, that's a good place to start," Bolt said as he took up the reins and nudged Nick into motion. "I wonder if there are any more scouts out here." He glanced to his right as Nick pulled out of the shadows of the trees. Just to make sure.

Bolt's heart leaped into his throat when he saw the fourth scout, not more than thirty feet away. The brave's eyes widened when he saw Bolt at the same instant.

The renegade scout yanked back on his reins, jerked his pony around the other way and took off at a gallop, riding away from Bolt.

Bolt started to go for his gun, knew instantly that a shot would bring the whole renegade band down on them. He acted fast. He couldn't let the scout get back to camp. He slapped the reins across Nick's side.

"Go, boy," he said as his horse took off at a dead run.

Tom and Veronica turned at the sound of his voice, just as Bolt raced after the retreating scout.

Bolt rode fast along the high ridge, caught up with the scout just as the brave reached a path that led down the slope.

Bolt calculated the distance. With outstretched arms, he leaped from his horse onto the Comanche's back, tossed him sideways, and both men tumbled off the Indian pony and crashed to the ground with a loud thump. Locked together, they rolled over twice, both reaching for their respective knives.

Bolt broke away from the fierce, strong brave and snatched his knife out of its scabbard. He rolled over again, dodging the renegade's lunging attack, then jumped to his feet.

The Comanche twisted around, grunting with the effort, and whipped his own knife from his breechclout. He made another lunge toward his enemy. Bolt raised his knife, aimed for the heart. The scout ducked sideways just as Bolt stabbed with the glinting weapon. Blood spurted from the long, deep gash in the brave's arm. Bolt had missed his mark.

The scout stood in front of Bolt, legs spread, sweat glistening on his bronze body, his black hair straight and scraggly. His dark eyes glittered as he held his knife up, taunting Bolt with his movement. He stabbed at Bolt, nicked him across the arm. Blood stained Bolt's sleeve and the crimson spread like an opening flower.

Bolt slammed his shiny weapon down across the renegade's wrist, sliced a piece of flesh away, and blood poured from the wound.

Angered, the savage Comanche whacked back and forth at Bolt, keeping the white man away from him, striking when he could. Bolt fended him off with his own weapon. The only sounds were the whick-whick of the flailing knives, the grunts and groans, the whispered scuffle of their feet on the ground.

The Indian connected twice. He put a small slit across Bolt's forehead, not deep, but the wound bled worse than the arm wound. Blood spilled from Bolt's other wound, on the side of his hand.

Bolt held his knife shoulder high, the tip of the weapon pointed at the renegade. He watched the scout's movements, studied his rhythm. When the Indian raised his hand high to lash out again, Bolt slammed his knife into the brave's chest. It plunged in deep, struck the heart.

The Indian's mouth fell open in surprise. His knife tumbled from his clutches as he collapsed to the bloodied ground and went limp.

"Bolt! Bolt. Are you all right?" Veronica cried in a hushed voice as she rode up to the bloody scene. Tom rode up behind her, leading Bolt's horse by the reins.

"Stay back, Veronica," Bolt whispered harshly.

He crouched over the dead renegade and with a few quick slashes, he took the Indian's scalp. He carried the scalp with him as he walked over and leaned against his horse, his clothes spattered with blood, his lungs aching from exhaustion.

"Bolt, how could you do that?" Veronica cried. She stood beside him, her eyes wide with shock.

"I had to do it," he said after he caught his breath.

"I mean the scalp," she said. "Why? It's so brutal."

"I had to do it, Veronica. To save all of our lives. If the Comanches think a white man is on their track, they'll disappear like smoke, and we'll never find them again. I took the scalp the way a Pawnee does, from the back of the head instead of the front. They'll be looking for Pawnee."

Bolt looked around at each of the other three scouts. They had made some progress in their rounds, and continued to ride slowly.

"That third scout we spotted, that one over on the right, is coming around," he said. "We'd better get out of here."

"Are you going to keep the scalp?" Veronica asked as she twisted her face up.

"Only until I can throw it away or bury it."

The trio rode back to their original viewing position, tucked into the trees, and waited. From there they couldn't see the dead renegade, but Bolt knew they didn't need to. It wasn't much more than five minutes before they heard the shrill war cry and knew that the scout had discovered the scalped brave.

Bolt watched the slope, where he now knew there was a path down to the meadow. Within minutes he saw the scout racing down the hill, his arm held high in the air, his hand fisted, his high-pitched war cry haunting to Bolt's ears. Even before the scout got down the hill, the other braves had gathered in front of the large tepee in the middle.

"Look over there," Tom said. "The other two scouts are going down there, too."

"Good. Let's hope they all ride off together."

Bolt saw that each scout took a separate path as he sped down the slope to join the others.

Chief Standing Antelope stepped out of the big tepee and greeted the scout. There was no mistaking the chief, even from that distance. He wore a bonnet of red and black feathers, while the other braves wore only a single feather in their hair.

Gestures were made, by the scout who pointed up the hill, by the chief when he gave his orders. The renegades scattered to their tepees, emerged some minutes later, painted for war. They gathered once more in front of their chief, then mounted their ponies, rode up the slope and disappeared from sight.

"Where are they going?" Veronica asked.

"After Pawnee, I hope," Bolt said.

The camp was deserted except for the four squaws who stood by the kettles and watched their men go off to war.

"We'd better get down there while it's quiet," Bolt said.

"Bolt, I'm scared," Veronica said.

"It won't be so bad with the renegades gone," Bolt reassured her.

"It isn't that, Bolt. All this time I've been so sure Heather is down there. Now I'm scared she won't be."

"I know what you mean, Veronica. I feel the same way."

CHAPTER SEVENTEEN

"What's your plan?" Tom asked.

"We just sneak down there and hope to hell those squaws don't notice us while we're pawin' through their tepees lookin' for Heather," Bolt said. "Simple enough."

"I hope it goes that smoothly," Tom smiled.

"Where do you think she is, Bolt? In that big tepee in the middle?" Veronica asked.

"That's my first guess. If not, we'll go from there. Are you ready?"

Veronica took a deep breath. "Yes, I'm ready. Let's go and get it over with."

Bolt led the way, riding along the wide ledge until he came to the first path. He had gone left so they wouldn't have to pass by the dead Indian. Surefooted, Nick picked his way down the slope. On the way down, Bolt dodged the tree branches that hung too far out on the path.

The squaws were busy with their chores near the firepit and didn't notice them as Bolt and the others reached the bottom of the hill and started across the thick green meadow. Bolt rode between two of the tepees on the outer ring of the circle, with Veronica and Tom right behind him.

Bolt and his group were thirty feet from the firepit when one of the squaws finally looked up and noticed him. She said something in her native tongue and the other three women turned to stare. Bolt watched them carefully to see their reactions to the strangers in their camp.

Suddenly, one of the squaws turned and raced for a tepee. Not the chief's tepee, but the closest one to it. Bolt whipped out his pistol and shot her in the back. The squaw dropped to the ground, landed face down, and never moved again.

Veronica gasped. "Bolt! No! Don't kill the women," she cried.

Bolt turned his pistol on the other three squaws as they started to walk toward their fallen friend. The frightened women scattered and dashed to the safety of their tepees.

Bolt dropped down from his horse, walked over and looked down at the body.

"Why, Bolt?" Veronica said as she rode over closer. "Why would you kill an innocent woman?"

Bolt turned the woman over with his foot. She gripped a small cutting knife in her hand. Bolt had seen her snatch it up just before she raced toward the tepee. "Because your sister's in there, Veronica, and this woman meant to kill her. She knew all along why we came."

"I didn't know," Veronica said as she shook her

head. She slid down from her saddle and dashed over to the tepee. With Tom and Bolt behind her, she threw open the hide flap and stared inside. "Oh, my God," she said when she saw her sister.

Heather sat in a corner of the tepee, cowering, frightened, her eyes wide and glassy.

"Heather, what have they done to you?" Veronica dashed inside and grabbed up her sister, took her in her arms. She held the girl at arm's length and looked her.

"Veronica?" Heather said, her voice barely audible. "You're here, Veronica. You're here."

"Yes, I'm here, Heather. You're safe now." Veronica took her sister in her arms again and they hugged each other tightly.

"Oh, Veronica, thank God you've come," Heather cried. "I was so scared."

"Are you all right, Heather?"

Bolt heard the trilling mournful threnody and knew that the Comanche squaws had sneaked back out of their tepees and were mourning over the dead woman.

"We've got to go, girls," he said. "Before that caterwauling brings the Comanche braves back down on us."

"Take me home," Heather cried. "Please take me home."

Bolt snatched a bedroll from the floor, stuffed it under his arm. "Tom, ride over to the corral and get one of those Indian ponies for Heather to ride. Hurry, please. We've got to get out of here."

Within twenty minutes, the foursome was up the hill and back on the road to home. They didn't stop to rest for three more hours. Bolt wanted to put as much time and distance between his group and the Comanches as he possibly could. He just hoped the renegades took time to bury their dead before they went out on the warpath again.

"Tom, we're being followed," Bolt told his friend in mid-afternoon the following day.

"You sure, Bolt?" Tom looked back at their backtrail, but couldn't see any riders.

The two men were down at a stream, filling their canteens.

"I'm sure. I spotted the spiral of trail dust in the distance early this morning. Didn't pay much attention to it at the time. But I've kept my eye on it all day, whenever it was in sight."

"Standing Antelope and his renegade band?" Tom asked.

"I'm afraid so. They're gaining on us, Tom, and I finally got a glimpse of their war paint. Red and black."

"Are you going to tell Heather and Veronica?"

"Not yet. Not until I have to. Those girls have been through enough already. They don't need something else to worry about."

"What're we gonna do, Bolt?"

"Just keep riding. Stay off the main road if they get any closer. Watch our backtrail. We won't have any more campfires."

"Yeah, we'll have to be real careful from now on. How far back are they?"

"Half a day's ride, maybe more. I haven't seen them since noon."

"Damn," Tom said. "There's nothing out here but this great big prairie."

"Well, I wanted you to know so you could keep your eyes open."

The men carried the canteens back up to the horses, where the two girls sat on one of the blankets. Heather looked better, but Bolt was worried about her. There were times when her eyes glazed over and she looked like she was going crazy.

"Mount up, gals," he told them. "It's time to hit the trail."

Before Bolt mounted his saddle, he walked back and checked his backtrail. They were at a place where the plains stretched out for a long way behind them, the creek-rutted land covered with tall summer grasses, dotted by an occasional clump of trees. He was almost relieved to see the line of riders way back there on the horizon, so far away, he could barely distinguish the riders from their horses. He knew who they were, though.

Bolt sighed with relief. The band of renegade Comanches had dropped back a long way since he'd last spotted them before noon. Maybe Standing Antelope was tiring of the chase, he thought. Maybe the chief was ready to give it up.

Just before Bolt turned back to his horse, he

caught a glimpse of movement, about a mile back. Not on the trail itself, but off to his left, in the tall grasses, near a cluster of cotton-woods. Birds, maybe? Black crows or buzzards hunting for prey? He couldn't be sure. And then he saw it again, as the rider emerged out of a ravine in the high grass. "Damned scout," he muttered to himself.

"Tom, take the lead for a while," he said as the others mounted up. "I'll bring up the rear."

Tom gave him a quizzical look, but Bolt just shook his head and Tom took the lead. As they rode, Bolt dropped back from the others, then finally turned off the trail when he found a clump of thick trees off to the side. His rifle cocked and ready, he hid in the trees and waited for nearly ten minutes before the renegade scout surfaced on the landscape again. The rider was opposite him, on the other side of the road, too far away for a good shot. The Comanche scout was riding fast now.

Bolt knew now that he couldn't just pick him off as he rode by, as he'd planned. He had to go after him, stop him from catching up to Tom and the girls. "Hey, renegade! Over here." Bolt shouted at the same time he rode out from the trees, his rifle ready.

The scout reined up at the sound of Bolt's voice. When the brave saw Bolt riding toward him, the painted Indian let out a shrill warwhoop, snatched an arrow from his quiver, took aim as he raced toward the white man.

Before the Indian could let the arrow fly, the

crack of the rifle shot rang through the air. The force of the bullet knocked the brave backward and he tumbled off the back of his pony, crashed to the hard ground, dead from the bullet wound in his chest.

Bolt rode across the road and into the high grasses to make sure the scout was dead. When he was sure, Bolt dismounted and untied the rope that held the bloody scalp he'd taken earlier. He tossed the grotesque scalp on the dead scout's chest. And even though he knew that the sound of the rifle shot would cause Standing Antelope and his men to pick up their pace, Bolt took the time to do something else.

He gathered up a handful of small pebbles and walked over to the road. He arranged the pebbles in the shape of an antelope, in the middle of the road so the rock drawing wouldn't be missed by the approaching renegades. Before he climbed back on his horse, Bolt walked back to the dead Indian, snatched the single black, red-tipped feather from his hair. He stuck the feather into the heart of the drawing, then rode off. Maybe Standing Antelope would know that Bolt was willing to play his game if he had to.

Bolt caught up to his friends a few minutes later. After the rifle shot, they had stopped to wait for him on the road.

"What happened?" Veronica asked. "What was the shot?"

"Just killed a snake," Bolt told her with a smile. "Nothin' for you to concern yourself about."

"Bolt, what is going on?" Veronica demanded. "You've been acting strange all day, since early morning. I've never seen you so jumpy."

Bolt thought for a long moment, then decided that the girls had a right to know that they were being chased by the murdering Indians.

"The renegade Comanches are on our trail," he said calmly. "I just killed their scout."

"You mean those Indians are coming after us?" Heather said, her dark eyes full of fear.

"They're a long way back, Heather," Bolt told the frightened girl. "My guess is that they'll give up on the chase and turn back before long." Bolt studied the girl's face and thought how much she looked like her sister. The long, dark hair, the soft natural beauty of her face, the tall gracefulness in the way she carried herself. The difference between the girls now was that Heather had that same frightened, desperate, look in her eyes that Veronica had had when he'd first seen her. In time, he hoped the expression in Heather's eyes would soften, as Veronica's had.

"Bolt, can't we outrun them?" Veronica asked. "We could just ride as fast as we can until we're well away from them, until we lose them."

"We can't do that, Veronica," Bolt said.

"But we can't let them catch up to us. Heather and I can keep up the pace," Veronica begged.

"The horses can't," Bolt said.

"But we've got fast horses," she said.

"They'd get winded, Veronica, and we'd risk

having them drop dead on us. Then we'd be in a fine kettle. No, Veronica. The horses have to be kept at an even pace. A short burst of speed wouldn't hurt them, but we'll save that for a time when we need it."

"How many of them are there?" Tom asked. "Have they been close enough for you to count?"

"There are ten of them now, Tom," Bolt said. "Two are dead."

"I still don't like the odds," Tom muttered as he took up the reins and motioned for the others to follow him.

Two days went by and the Comanche renegades were closing the gap. Even though Bolt and his group stayed off the main road now, zigzagging across the prairie to leave a confusing trail, the Indians pushed on. The last time Bolt had spotted them, they were close enough for him to make out the individual riders. They were close enough for Bolt to see that Chief Standing Antelope, wearing his feather bonnet, rode at the head of the line.

Bolt had managed to kill three more scouts who had been sent out ahead of the band. He killed them in much the same manner as he'd killed the other one. And always, Bolt left the pebble drawing in the middle of the road, the black and red feathers of the dead brave stuck in the heart of the antelope-shaped arrangement of pebbles.

The lonesome prairie stretched on forever and

there was no place for Bolt and his group to go, except to keep on riding, trying to shake the Indians from their trail.

At the rate the Comanches were closing in on them, Bolt knew that they would be facing a showdown soon. Probably by noon the next day.

CHAPTER EIGHTEEN

The showdown came earlier than Bolt had figured. And it came when he was least expecting it.

Bolt and the others had ridden well into the night, stopping for only a couple of hours to rest, before they hit the trail again well before dawn. When the first light of morning finally spilled across the land, Bolt had stopped long enough to thoroughly scan their backtrail. During the next two hours, he had paused every fifteen minutes to look over the land, scrutinizing the creek-rutted plains as far as he could see, in all directions.

He saw absolutely no sign of the Comanche renegades that morning. No trail dust rising in the air in the distance, no flashes of movements. No scouts sent out ahead of the others, as had been Standing Antelope's custom.

Figuring that the Comanches had finally tired of the chase and turned back, Bolt took the lead again as they rode through the uneven, scarred land. Land that had been ravaged years before by flooding waters that had left deep gulleys and ravines in its wake.

Bolt had taken his group back to the regular

trail where the going was easier. He was just beginning to relax in the saddle when he looked out at the road ahead and saw the band of renegade Comanche coming up over the horizon. There were seven of them, and they were riding straight for Bolt, charging at full bore, bows in hand, arrows ready to be set in place.

Damn, the Indians must have ridden all night in order to circle Bolt's group and charge them from the front. Bolt hadn't disregarded that possibility and had, in fact, checked the landscape ahead of them every time he'd stopped to look. But the renegades had disappeared completely from sight that morning and now they came charging toward Bolt's group, like ghosts out of the past.

Bolt glanced around and quickly studied the landscape. He saw that Tom and Heather and Veronica had all noticed the fast-approaching attackers. Panic rippled across Veronica's face, but Heather just sat in her saddle, a dazed look on her face, her eyes vacant.

"Dismount," Bolt ordered as he slipped down from his saddle and grabbed the rifle that rested across the pommel. "Take your rifles. Hide in that creek bed over there," he said as he pointed.

The girls did as they were told, although Tom had to help Heather along. She seemed confused, as if she were in a fog and didn't know what was happening.

The Comanches barreled down on them, their wild war cries piercing Bolt's ears.

"Stay down," Bolt cautioned the others. "Don't shoot until I tell you to."

Heather cracked under the noise of the pounding hoofbeats, the shrill, taunting war cries. She stood up suddenly, screaming like a mad woman, in full view of the Indians. She tried to scramble up out of the ravine. An arrow whizzed by her head just as Tom pulled her back down.

Bolt raised up briefly, fired a shot, knocked the closest brave off his horse. The brave crashed to the ground, a big bullet hole in his heart.

The shooting began as the braves discarded their bows and arrows and took up their own rifles. The Comanches made a pass at the ravine, shooting down at the others. Bolt stood and picked off another brave as he reloaded his weapon. Tom took out another brave at the same time.

The Comanches rode away and then turned and made another run on the ravine. Again Bolt waited until after the braves had fired their shots and were reloading. Tom killed another Comanche as Bolt raised up quickly and blew a brave away with one shot. Bolt whirled around and, with his repeating rifle, he shot at a nearby Comanche before the brave could reload.

The wounded renegade tumbled from his horse and rolled down into the ravine, ended up right next to Veronica, who was too startled to move away. Wounded only in the upper thigh, the brave brought out his knife, raised it above Veronica, was ready to plunge it into the girl's heart. Heather snapped to her senses. She raised her rifle, took aim, and shot a big hole in the brave's back before he could slam the knife into Veronica.

Heather broke into hysterical sobs after she killed the man. Tom and Bolt turned to help the girls.

When Standing Antelope realized he was all alone in his pursuit, that the rest of his band were dead, he swung around and made a hasty retreat.

Veronica scrambled up out of the ravine, her rifle still clutched in her hand. When she saw the renegade chief riding away, her eyes filled with hatred. She raised her rifle, took careful aim, and pulled the trigger. Her bullet smashed into the back of Standing Antelope's head. The chief's feathered bonnet shot straight up in the air as brain matter exploded from the skull. Standing Antelope toppled from his horse, landed face up, his arms and legs twisted at grotesque angles. The red and black feathered bonnet floated down and settled on his chest.

Bolt walked over and looked down at the dead chief. "You got your feather, Standing Antelope, but you lost the game."

Veronica came up beside him. "Is he dead?"

"Yes, Veronica. It's all over now."

"I don't know if it'll ever be over, Bolt. The scars from this nightmare will always be there."

"Things will get better, in time."

Veronica shook her head sadly. "I wonder if Heather will ever recover from the effects of this whole tragic ordeal. She's been through so much more than the rest of us."

Bolt looked at Veronica and smiled. "She's a Morningstar. She'll recover." He put his arm around the trembling girl and led her away.

The foursome rounded up their horses and without looking back at the bloody battlefield, they rode away. Wanting to get as far away from the bad memories as they could, they stayed in the saddle all day long.

It was almost dark when they finally stopped to make camp. Exhausted, they climbed down from their mounts. While Bolt and Tom built a small fire and prepared a small stew from the foot in their saddlebags, the girls sat on a blanket near the fire. Veronica comforted her sister and assured her that their mother and Aunt Sophie were fine, that they were being well taken care of at Bolt's ranch. She told Heather that when they got back to the ranch, the four Morningstar women would leave the ranch and start a new life for themselves.

After supper, they were sitting around the fire, talking about other things, when Heather suddenly burst into tears.

"I can't stand it any more," she cried. "No! No! I can't bear it." Her body heaved with great sobs.

Tom, who was sitting next to her, put his arm around her. "It's all right now, Heather. You're safe. Nobody'll hurt you again."

"It won't go away," she cried hysterically. "It's all I can think of."

"What did they do to you?" Tom asked.

"Everything," Heather cried. "It was horrible."

"All of them?"

"Yes. The women were the worst. They beat me and kicked me. They made me grovel for scraps of food."

"What about the men?" Tom asked. "Did they hurt you?"

Heather stared into the fire, her eyes flashing with hatred. "Yes," she said. "They humiliated me. They stripped me of my dignity. They took me against my will. All of them. Their chief, Standing Antelope, was brutal to me." She turned and collapsed into Tom's arms, weeping, shuddering.

"It's all right now," Tom said as he stroked her hair. "Nobody's going to hurt you any more."

"Things will get better, Heather, I promise," Veronica said from across the fire, where she snuggled close to Bolt.

"I'm so scared," Heather cried. "I don't want to close my eyes tonight because it will all come back to me. All of the horror, the pain."

Tom pulled her close. "I'll take care of you tonight," he said gently. "I'll hold you all night long. Nothing will hurt you."

"You can feel safe with Bolt and Tom," Veronica said to her sister. "They're the kindest, most gentle and compassionate men I've ever known."

Bolt squeezed Veronica. "Thank you, Veronica," he said with a crooked grin. "I didn't know you felt that way about me."

She looked up at him with a teasing smile.

"You're lucky, Bolt."

"How's that?"

"If I didn't need to get on with my life, I just might stick around your ranch and nag you until you married me. I think you'd make a fine husband."

"Yeah, I guess I'm pretty lucky at that," he grinned.

"Oh, you!" Veronica gave him a playful slap on the shoulder, then snuggled into his arms. "I think it's bedtime."

"Good idea."

It was after dark when they finally arrived at the Rocking Bar Ranch the following night. They rode straight to the bordello so Heather could be reunited with her mother and Aunt Sophie. The bordello was bright with lights. The din of laughter and music and boisterous voices spilled out of the log cabin.

"Judging from the noise, it must be Saturday night," Tom commented as he helped Heather down from the Indian pony.

"What's going on here?" Heather asked, her eyes wide with curiosity as she stared up at the house. "Are they having a party?"

"Never mind, Heather," Veronica said with a smile. "I'll explain it all to you in the morning."

The foursome headed up the steps. Veronica stopped halfway up. "I don't believe it," she said.

"What don't you believe?" Bolt asked.

"That's Mama!"

"Where?" Heather asked, looking up at the open door where she could see the crowded smoke-filled room. "I don't see her."

"That's Mama playing the piano," Veronica said. "I don't believe it."

"Yes, that is Mama playing," Heather said as she stopped to listen. "I recognize the song from church, but it sounds different somehow." Heather dashed on up the stairs.

The others followed her. Heather pushed through the crowd of boisterous men, ignoring them, as she made her way to the piano. She patted her mother on the shoulder.

Bolt saw the look of shock on Bertha's face when she saw her lost daughter. Bertha jumped up from the piano stool and threw her arms around Heather and the two embraced for a long time, tears streaming down their faces.

"Heather's going to be all right now," Bolt sighed. "Your mother can get her through the bad times."

"Oh, no! I don't believe it," Veronica said.

"What?" Bolt asked.

"Look at Aunt Sophie. Just look at that fancy gown she's wearing. And the rouge on her face. Do you suppose . . . no, she couldn't be."

Sophie spotted them from across the room. She set the tray she was carrying down on a nearby table and rushed over to them.

"Did you find Heather?" Sophie asked as she wrapped her arms around Veronica and squeezed her.

"Yes. She's over there with Mama," Veronica nodded.

"Oh, thank God," Sophie said as she released Veronica. "I want to go see her." She turned away and started toward the piano.

Veronica tugged on her aunt's arm.

"Aunt Sophie, you're not . . . you're not working here, are you?"

"Yes, I'm working here. Bertha's working here, too. We have been all this week."

"Mama, too?" Veronica cried. "How could you? How could Mama? I can't believe it."

"It's not what you think, Veronica," Sophie laughed when she saw the shocked look on Veronica's face. "Mama plays the piano every night. And I serve drinks to the gentlemen. Nothing more. Oh, I've kind of been thinking about doing what the other girls do, but Harmony won't let me."

"I'm glad to hear that," Veronica sighed. "Is Harmony here? I'd like to meet her after all that I've heard about her."

"She's here," Sophie said. "She's the madam."

"The madam?" Veronica looked up at Bolt, an accusing look in her eyes. "I thought she cleaned and cooked for you."

"She does," Bolt smiled. "Harmony does a lot of things around here. I already told you that."

"Harmony's over there with Bertha and Heather, Sophie said. "Come on, let's go over there."

Bolt and Veronica followed Sophie through the crowd and the four Morningstar women hugged each other joyously. Bolt finally introduced Veronica to Harmony.

"I've heard a lot about you," Veronica said politely as she eyed the pretty, buxom blonde.

"You have a good family here," Harmony smiled. "And I'm so glad you found your sister. We've all been worried about her, and all of you."

"Thank you for taking care of Mama and Aunt Sophie."

"I enjoyed having them here," Harmony said. "If you'll excuse me, I've got customers banging on the bar. I'd better get back over there." Harmony walked away.

"Isn't it wonderful?" Bertha said as she hugged Veronica again. "Harmony let us work here while you were gone. Your Aunt Sophie and I have already earned enough money so we can go on to San Antonio and find a place to settle down. Harmony said the people in town would help us find work. Now that you and Heather are back, we Morningstars can finally start a new life for ourselves."

"I'm glad, Mama, but I'm going to miss this place," Veronica said as she looked around the room. "It's been home to us."

"I know. I'll miss it, too." Bertha turned to Bolt. "Thank you, Bolt, for everything you've done for us. And I like your friends. They're all perfect gentlemen around me." She stood on her tiptoes and gave him a kiss on the cheek. And then she stepped back over to hug Heather again.

"Well, life is full of surprises," Bolt said as he rubbed his cheek.

"Yes, it is," Veronica said as she looked up at Bolt.

"Does Harmony take care of your other needs, too?" Veronica asked with a sly look. "I thought you didn't sleep with the whores."

"Harmony isn't one of the whores, Veronica. She's the madam."

"Well, do you? Do you sleep with Harmony?"

"You ask too many questions, Veronica," Bolt said with a teasing smile.

THE UNTAMED WEST
brought to you by Zebra Books

ILLINOIS PRESCOTT   (2142, $2.50)
by G. Clifton Wisler

Darby Prescott was just fourteen when he and his family left Illinois and joined the wagon train west. Ahead lay endless miles of the continent's rawest terrain . . . and as Cheyenne war whoops split the air, Darby knew the farmboy from Illinois had been left behind, and whatever lay ahead would be written in hot lead and blood.

TOMBSTONE LODE   (1915, $2.95)
by Doyle Trent

When the Josey mine caved in on Buckshot Dobbs, he left behind a rich vein of Colorado gold — but no will. James Alexander, hired to investigate Buckshot's self-proclaimed blood relations learns too soon that he has one more chance to solve the mystery and save his skin or become another victim of TOMBSTONE LODE.

LONG HENRY   (2155, $2.50)
by Robert Kammen

Long Henry Banner was marshal of Waco and a confirmed bachelor — until the day Cassandra stepped off the stagecoach. A week later they were man and wife. And then Henry got bushwhacked by a stranger and when he was back on his feet, his new wife was gone. It would take him seven years to track her down . . . to learn her secret that was sealed with gunpowder and blood!

GALLOWS RIDERS   (1934, $2.50)
by Mark K. Roberts

When Stark and his killer-dogs reached Colby, all it took was a little muscle and some well-placed slugs to run roughshod over the small town — until the avenging stranger stepped out of the shadows for one last bloody showdown.

DEVIL WIRE   (1937, $2.50)
by Cameron Judd

They came by night, striking terror into the hearts of the settlers. The message was clear: Get rid of the devil wire or the land would turn red with fencestringer blood. It was the beginning of a brutal range war.

Available wherever paperbacks are sold, or order direct from the Publisher. Send cover price plus 50¢ per copy for mailing and handling to Zebra Books, Dept. 2265, 475 Park Avenue South, New York, N.Y. 10016. Residents of New York, New Jersey and Pennsylvania must include sales tax. DO NOT SEND CASH.